Jones Barnett

Edited by Harriett Barnett Ford

Kinta Storyteller Blends History, Ghostly Tales, (and pulls a few tails)

For Family Fun on Stormy Nights

ISBN: 1-4392-4305-0
ISBN-13: 9781439243053

To order additional copies, please contact us.
BookSurge
www.booksurge.com
1-866-308-6235
orders@booksurge.com

DEDICATION

This book is dedicated to the Barnett family and all the good, the bad, and the ugly people of Kinta, Oklahoma. (Actually, I never met a Kinta person I didn't like, and not one of them is ugly.)

Like Mark Twain stated in his forward to *Tom Sawyer*, I challenge anyone to find a semblance of plot in the following pages. The characters are drawn from life, real or imagined. You will have to decide which is which.

Kinta readers will find amusement, a little history, whether it happened or not, and probably some things to fuss, discuss, and even cuss about.

Now I dare you to turn the first page.

PROLOGUE

A warning before you begin . . .

Do You Believe in Ghosts?
By Jones Barnett (1918-1994)

I must begin by saying there's nothing to be scared about if you should run into a ghost. These things still happen, regardless of who says they don't.

I saw one the other day while walking home in the deepening twilight from Sans Bois creek bottom. The old spook didn't look too scary. He just walked along beside me and even joined in singing a little tune I happened to be whistling at the time. I never missed a note. Just kept on whistling.

Guess I can't find anything to get scared about anymore. However, I can certainly tell a tale or two that might scare you.

I'll even include a little history and homespun wit, and wisdom, such as was often discussed by Kinta folks over Lilly Belle Mizell's café tables through the years, as well as over my own.

If this happens to be the proverbial dark and story night, read at your own risk.

1

Stalled in A Storm
The following short story is printed in a collection titled *I Never Believed in Ghosts Until . . .* **compiled and released in 1992 by USA Weekend Contemporary Books**

Does any evidence exist of actual spirit beings? The kind most folks call a ghost? John Steinbeck once said, "I do not believe in ghosts although I have seen them."

I believe thoroughly in them, although I have *never* seen one.

My strange encounter happened during a stall in a wild snow storm that could have been fatal for my family. It was the winter of 1948. I was traveling through the northwestern states in my old 1939 Plymouth coupe with my wife, my two-year old daughter, and not much else.

Whistling wind swished curtains of dry snow across the streets of Denver as I paid the service station attendant for filling the tank of our old Plymouth coupe. He added some anti-freeze to the carburetor and also a quart of oil. The fellow noticed my license tag with the bucking horse emblem and said, "If you're looking for a place to put up for the night there's a motel just down the highway about a half mile from here on your right."

I thanked him and got back inside the Plymouth.

My wife and daughter were comfortably warm with blankets tucked around them, even though a scant amount of air fanned out from the Plymouth's little heater.

I was young and not long discharged from military service. Like many other soldiers returning from winning the war, I believed myself thoroughly competent to accomplish anything I set out to do.

My primary reason for not staying in Denver that night was that I had to spend money to keep the Plymouth running. It had fuel pump problems in Buffalo and carburetor problems in Lamar, Colorado. There was just enough money left to make it the rest of the way to Sheridan, Wyoming.

I took the chance, and pulled onto the snowy highway. I still wonder about that decision, taking my family's lives in my hands. The snow whitened my windshield, blowing up from the highway in a sweeping arc. Visibility was barely fifteen feet, and even less at times.

I thought I'd soon be able to see better when we left the glare of city lights. I could not.

I considered turning back, but thought of my thin wallet and convinced myself the storm had to let up after a while.

Either that or we'll drive out of it.

I kept on driving slowly to avoid a skid, doing thirty miles per hour. There was no other traffic on the wind-whipped roads, so I didn't have to worry about much except keeping the little coupe on the slippery highway.

Visibility became so bad at times I would have to make a complete stop and clear the packed snow from the windshield. My wife and baby slept soundly, but I was too strained to feel the drowsiness that comes with late-night driving. A glance at my watch told me it was after one a.m.

I don't suppose we had traveled more than a hundred miles from Denver when the tiny heater just couldn't keep the cold at bay any more. The car grew uncomfortably cold. Visibility became less than a foot. Instead of driving out of the storm, we were smack in the middle of a raging, white-out. I could not even see if the coupe had strayed into the on-coming traffic lane. If we were to meet a trucker, the driver surely would not see us until it was too late. We would likely be hit.

I stopped the coupe, opened my door, and stepped out on the highway to determine where the center lane was. Then I managed to pull over onto the right side of the road. A sudden gust of wind shook the car like a toy.

Why hadn't I stayed in Denver?

I could have called my boss for the money.

Man this was dumb. I raced the motor a little in order to increase the heat output. The engine coughed, sputtered, and quit altogether.

It refused to turn over.

I sat there, shaken more by my thoughts than by the cold. How long could we survive in this sub-zero weather? Sure stay in the car, everyone knows that. But how many people are found frozen to death inside cars on the morning after a blizzard?

My wife awoke and asked, "What happened?"

"Carburetor flooded again. I'll fix it," I answered with false confidence.

I couldn't fix it, and I knew it. "I'm going to wait till this wind lets up a little," I stalled.

She replied, "You can fix it," and pulled the blankets tighter around herself and the baby, closing her eyes again.

I sat there at a complete loss. What to do? I was no auto mechanic. The bone-chilling cold started creeping in, and I shivered, very aware of our desperate situation. We had not seen another vehicle on the road in miles.

Then I heard a sound above the howling wind. I roused myself and listened. There it was again. Someone tapping at the window. I strained to see through the night-black glass. No car. No headlights behind or ahead.

Impossibly, the hood of my Plymouth rose. *It has to be the wind*, I said to myself. I've got to get out and close the hood before a gust tears it away. As I climbed out, I saw a shadowy image—a *figure* bent over the front of the car, peering under the hood. I could hear the sound of a screwdriver and a wrench. Then the hood lowered.

A voice said, "Try it now. Try your starter." I got back in the car and did as told. The little engine sputtered to life and picked up a rhythm. I looked out my door to offer my thanks and saw no one.

No one was there.

I pulled the stick shift into first gear, let out the clutch and forged ahead into the elements.

We traveled safely the whole night through, even though we passed several vehicles in the ditches near the towns. When my wife next opened her eyes, I had parked in front of a combination service station and all-night café. We got out and went inside for breakfast.

The snowplows were out in full force on the highway, clearing the snow and picking up stranded travelers. Soon we were back on the road.

By nightfall we made it safely to Sheridan. Not until then did my wife say to me, "You know I never knew you to be able to fix anything. But you did come through in an emergency, didn't you?"

I muttered, "I guess when I had to, I was able enough."

I don't know if I ever told her the entire story.

Strange things have happened on the roads.

On a similar, but less mysterious note, one day in 1967, I had just purchased a new sport model Chevrolet. I was excited to show this wonderful automobile to my wife, but when I arrived home she had to interrupt my jubilation with some sad news. Our aunt, a widow with very few relatives, was hospitalized that day with a heart condition. It was our duty to visit her in Tulsa.

"Okay! Let's be off," I said eager for the chance to drive my new car. (Of course I was concerned about our aunt too.)

As we loaded for the trip, Christine asked, "Have you checked this car for tools that you might need in case of car problems?"

"No need," I answered. When I purchased the car I had immediately installed a set of the best tires, replacing the ones that came with it. For some reason I still don't understand, a lug wrench or a jack had not come with the car. I knew this, but assured Christine, "The new tires have a 50,000-mile guarantee, so not to worry." I didn't bother to remove any tire tools from our other car parked behind the house.

About eight miles out of Okmulgee, I heard a rumm-mmm, buzzzz, thunkety-thunk, and the car veered shakily to the right. I fought to bring it to a stop out of the path of traffic.

Sure enough. A blow out.

I just sat there and condemned my foolish risk-taking. I hadn't even climbed out of the car when another driver pulled up behind me. I couldn't see his face because darkness had set in. In moments, the fellow had a jack under the axle and had pulled off the wheel.

I raised the trunk, pulled out the spare, and picked up the flat tire. He tightened the lug bolts.

Before I had time to thank him, the stranger got back in his car, made a u-turn, and drove away in the *opposite* direction.

Where had he been headed before my blow out?

All I know is that he drove up with tire tools when I truly needed help. He wasn't a ghost, because if he was then some ghosts have to be black. I still wish I had written to the local newspaper in Okmulgee to express my thanks and appreciation for what that man did.

A ghost? No way. But what? Luck? I'd say more than that.

A few times in my life, I've been given the opportunity to help others in need, but I don't believe the above encounters were rewards for my own service.

There are simply times when someone appears on the scene to do a much-needed service for another. These visitations may be labeled spirits or even angels by believers, while skeptics explain them away.

Steinbeck did not believe in ghosts. Neither do I, however I think I know very well what it was that he saw.

Back When

Everyone looks back from time to time. There's a lot of reminiscing in these pages, so you might as well get ready for it. If you don't enjoy looking back, you haven't lived long enough.

When I was a kid, I sometimes listened to my Mom read a letter from a relative. Below is the old style of writing that Kinta people once learned from formal composition books.

"On this 22nd day of March, in the year of our Lord, 1990, I take pen in hand to inform you of the latest happenings in our area."

See, I bored you already.

Now to get the attention of the reader and arouse interest, I always thought one should begin a letter with a bit of drama. I also thought an interesting story should begin something like the following.

Phantom Hitchhiker

There was a faint and distant rumble of thunder in the southlands, and the dim glow of lightning from inside the bellies of lowering clouds. The storm had been approaching slowly, clearly visible from the south all evening.

I turned the radio dial to the weather station as I drove through heavily timbered lands on narrow country roads. My assistant and I had been surveying in unfamiliar territory and we wouldn't get home before morning.

My main concern at the time was staying on the correct road leading to the little mountain resort area where my helper, Jack, and I hoped to get rooms for the night.

The wind picked up, gusting with fierce intensity. Thunder clapped more frequently, and the lightning became a constant flicker. At brief intervals the darkened countryside lit up as bright as day. Pelting rain started slapping the car in wind-driven sheets. The wipers could scarcely keep the windshield clear enough for me to see the narrow lane.

A weather report warned of flashfloods and mentioned the very area we were driving through.

"Well, not to worry," I assured Jack. "If we're on the wrong road, we have plenty of gas, and we'll eventually come out on a highway."

But as the rain came down harder, I had to shift down to first gear in order to keep moving. Yes, I was starting to get a bit worried. We had been on a long, descending curve down a sloping mountain for some while and now were headed into the river bottoms where rain-filled ruts were barely visible. At times we were forced to stop and back up to get enough traction to make it through the mud.

My old Ford was barely moving when the yellow wand of headlights bounced off an eerie shape sloshing and struggling through knee-deep water in the middle of the road. The figure made no effort to move to either side of the lane, and I couldn't get around it, so I honked my horn.

Whatever possessed a person to be out walking on such a wild, stormy night?

As I drew nearer, I could discern the figure was a woman. She stopped and faced my car. I rolled down my window, stuck my head out into the wind and rain, and yelled at her to approach the car and get in out of the storm.

Jack said, "For crying out loud, don't pick that woman up. Anyone out on a night like this has got to be nuts, or a maniac!"

He had spoken too late. The woman had already opened the back door of the car and was climbing inside.

She spoke not a word, so we proceeded in an uncomfortably strained silence, barely nodding to her. We approached a rickety bridge. I could see the rushing, storm-swollen waters, already lapping at the girders.

"Should we try it?" I asked.

"Don't pull onto that bridge," Jack insisted. "You can tell that it's getting ready to go."

Our passenger offered no comment.

I could see water rising, but I was determined to make it across.

For the second time that night, I ignored Jack's advice.

"I'm going ahead. I think it'll hold." I inched the Ford onto the unsteady structure. Jack held his breath and clenched his fists into white-knuckled balls.

We barely reached the other side when the bridge started disappearing under the roiling torrent. Jack called me seven kinds of names for taking the risk, but we made it across, so why get excited now?

The wind soon died to a steady but cold breeze, and the moon appeared from behind drained and empty clouds.

The storm had passed on, moving toward the North. I pulled up to a stop sign and a paved highway. With a glad sigh, I drove onto the empty lane and saw a welcome road sign. We were just two miles from the inn. I could see the relief on Jack's face.

As I glanced to the backseat to ask our silent passenger where she wanted to get out, a jolt of disbelief whipped through me.

We did *not have* a passenger.

I must admit I was shook up, as was Jack, who happened to be a highly nervous and sensitive being. He started to rattle a bit incoherently and cut loose with a nervous, high-pitched giggle. He then proceeded to condemn me to all eternity for giving a ride to one of "the devil's own."

I don't know who she was, but under those circumstances, I couldn't very well leave a lady to flounder in the dark at the mercy of the raging tempest, especially when I couldn't get around her.

But isn't that the case with any female?

You can't get around them.

Editor's note:

Over the years, a version of this story has become legend in different parts of the country. When Jones' daughter, Harriett Barnett Ford, (that's me) was teaching school in McAlester, Oklahoma during the early 1970s, a toll-booth attendant said more than a few white-faced motorists told of a vanishing hitchhiker they had picked up on a rain-soaked night along the Indian Nations turnpike.

The hiker sometimes spoke a cryptic warning about the end of the world coming soon. When the driver later glanced toward his passenger, he found only a pool of rain water on the seat.

Many of these travelers were credible members of the community. One of them was a state trooper.

There are variations of the legend; however the basic tale usually involves a beautiful woman on a roadway at night, described as dripping wet regardless of the weather.

One of the most famous phantom hitchhikers is known as Resurrection Mary, said to haunt the town of Justice, Illinois, a suburb of Chicago.

The driver stops to offer her a ride, and she gives him her address. When he arrives, the car is empty. Residents of the house greet him and say this happens to motorists every year on the anniversary of Mary's death.

The shocked driver learns how beautiful Mary died in an accident at the location where he first saw her. He sees a photo of the girl and recognizes her as the same woman he picked up.

Sometimes the driver visits Mary's grave and finds a jacket draped over her tombstone. The same jacket he had loaned to the wet, shivering girl when she climbed in the car.

There is no definite record of a young woman answering Mary's description as having been buried in Resurrection Cemetery, according to the burial register.

"With most men, unbelief in one thing springs from blind belief in another. A challenge to either presumption can lead to the discovery of Truth." Anonymous

Back Then

When I was a kid, exciting entertainment consisted of sitting around and listening to tales told by the older folks. I remember the poems of James Whitcomb Riley, and think of how we would sit around the kitchen fire and have the 'mostest' fun.

In my youth, society had changed so little from the days of *Little Orphan Annie* that my family practically lived those times in their exactness. When the supper was finished and the adults retired to the living room. A rosy glow radiated from the dying embers of coals in the kitchen stove. We had the kitchen all to ourselves and plenty of time before bed to spin yarns and frighten the younger kids. Visitors too.

We always had visitors. Why? I don't know, because we kids made it a point to make their stay miserable by scaring the dickens out of them. You see, I knew every scary tale in the book and I could spread the suspense on thick. But instead of discouraging our visitors, they always came back for more.

Devilish Fun?

Young Stu Edwards was a regular guest at our farmhouse. Stu had to walk home in the dark along a mountain trail after the spook-story session, and he'd complain to his father that he got so scared he had to run all the way home and nearly passed out from fright. This was his explanation for jumping into bed with his mom and dad and disturbing their sleep.

Stu's dad once complained to my folks that it was "un-Christian like" to tell stories about spirits, demons and things from the dark world. He insisted, "Those things are of the devil, and if you persist in playing around with such thoughts and devilish games you are leaving an open invitation for evil spirits to enter."

Now let me tell you this. I never took such things as evil spirits seriously. But I can relate to you something I witnessed that literally made me do a bit of re-thinking about what that gentleman said.

This is the whole truth. If it were not, it would not be worth telling.

My daughter was home after her first six weeks of college to spend the weekend. A game that was popular among the freshmen that year was the Ouija Board—some foolishness about pretending to call up spirits from beyond.

As far as calling up spirits, I did not give it any credence and was completely uninterested in what my daughter, her younger cousin, and her brother were up to. I was sitting apart from these kids, reading a Max Brand western when I noticed a low, murmuring rhythm of voices chanting, "Rise table, rise."

This chanting went on for perhaps four or five minutes, and I was about to give an order for it to stop, when I looked over toward them and (I can swear this to be true) the table was standing up on two legs. The other two legs were at least a foot above the floor. When the kids stopped chanting, the table dropped to the floor.

What caused that table to rise?

I am an engineer and work with the various sciences, geometry and math. I believe things move only by the force of man-created energy. That table moved by word command if you will.

Well, back to Stu. He swore to his dad that while walking home from our house one night, a spectral figure joined him at the footbridge across the creek on the mountain trail. The ghostly thing walked beside him for several steps and said not a word. Neither did Stu. His tongue cleaved to the roof of his mouth. He was too frightened even to run.

Before it departed, the figure's eyes glowed red as it handed him a piece of wood. Stu claimed the wood was smoking hot and said he had blisters on his hand to show to his dad when he finally got home that night, shaking and white faced.

Stu's father hit the ceiling and told my folks to see that I kept my mouth shut and not tell Stu any more frightening tales again.

Of course I was just a kid myself at the time and believed not one word of the ghost stories I'd heard. I thought Stu's experience was purely imaginative, a laughable yarn, and I was greatly amused by it. Still am.

However years later, after watching the performance of that table rising, I could almost agree with Stu's father, who was a Baptist minister.

I did not see Stu for a long while. Not till I was in my seventies and much too old for such foolishness.

It was about a year ago. Stu and I ran into each other and sat down to enjoy talking about the proverbial good old times of our long-ago youth. When you are old, all times are good.

I mentioned how I still regretted causing his father such concern over telling him ghostly tales and frightening him.

Stu chuckled and said, "You know, Jones, my Dad was right. He told me to never to dwell on demonic things. He said an evil spirit could enter you if you let your guard down."

"You really believe that?" I asked.

"Yes I do, and I can tell you why," he replied.

"I don't want to know why. You're my friend, Stu. Please don't. The time for ghost stories is over. We're adults and no longer find a thrill in scary things. Anyway, I don't believe in spirits or any such thing," I insisted.

"They exist," he returned.

"Well then, tell me this. If these evil spirits are in existence, why don't angelic spirits make themselves evident?"

Stu peered at me with a knowing glance. "I seem to recall you telling me about a figure on a road one night while you were stranded in a dangerous snow storm. The way I recollect, he started the motor on your old '39 model Plymouth coupe, making it possible for you to drive your wife and baby through mountain passes and snow drifts to Sheridan, Wyoming."

I had to admit I did recall that eerie event, and in fact will never forget it.

"How do you explain that?" Stu asked.

"I can't explain it, and I can assure you no one else can, but it must be explainable," I answered.

"It is explainable," Stu said, "When you recognize there are spirits from the other side, both angels and demons."

"Then why do we make such a big deal out of Halloween? Isn't that celebrating a night for evil spirits to come straight out of Hell?" I asked.

"Well, yes, actually it used to be just that." Stu agreed.

"If that's so, then how can we expect any consideration from angelic spirits to come from the heavenly realm? Haven't we insulted them by celebrating Halloween?" I looked at Stu in exasperation.

"We people aren't really too smart," he pondered. "We like thrills and adventure. Those among us who seek to contact the spirit world's darker side always manage to do so. Demons love to perform devilish tricks, and what they like best is to deceive people into thinking they're merely harmless, playful entities. That they're really something other than devils out to divert us from knowing the Truth. They love convincing poor, deluded people into thinking they've contacted lost relatives and departed spirits."

"Stu, what do you think your Dad would say about all this?" I asked, at last willing to consider what I had previously dismissed as nonsense. "Are people in serious trouble because they celebrate Halloween?" I was still having a hard time accepting this concept.

Stu spoke pleasantly. "My dad believed that although we shouldn't tamper with evil spirits, we could possibly be excused for an ignorant brush with the darker side. I suppose if we only think of Halloween as a joke, then we're not too far out in enemy territory."

I could see his point. We're not intentionally honoring old Slew Foot on Halloween. So let the spooks have their night. I suppose they deserve it, since our nation believes in equal opportunity and absolutely no discrimination.

Equal opportunity for demons? Now that's an interesting thought.

I am deciding at this time to go out, clean the pumpkin, carve a frightful face on it, set a candle inside, and scare the dickens out of some hapless people.

If anyone gets too upset, I'll just say the devil did it. That excuse worked well when I was a child and Aunt Belle used to ask me who dipped his fingers in the frosting on the cake. Of course I never thought she actually believed there was a real devil any more than a real Santa Claus.

Now. . . I wonder.

Angels and demons. I doubted once, however I think perhaps I've met a few of each.

Editor's note:

Some groups get all worked up about Halloween, a festival which had its origins in ancient Celtic and Druidic traditions to mark the end of the autumn harvest on October 31.

Why? Long ago, many people believed the barrier could be crossed between the worlds of the living and the dead, the satanic as well as the sacred, on All Hallows Eve. The Day of the Dead is still celebrated with skeletal masks and costumes in many cultures.

In the seventh century, Pope Boniface IV introduced All Saint's Day to replace the Roman Feralia, a pagan event for the dead. Over the years, the two festivals somehow merged into one event on Halloween.

In America, Halloween is looked at simply as a night for kids in costumes knocking on doors for a candy handout.

For most people, the night has no connection with thoughts of the dead or evil spirits.

My thought is this. Even if it were a night totally dedicated to Satanic worship by those so inclined, Christian people can certainly reclaim the date and celebrate it for the Lord. Why let the devil steal any night for his own?

Having said that, I would not play around with the Ouija board, horoscopes, or table tapping today. Not after reading Deut. 18: 9-12 and numerous other biblical warnings against contacting the spirit world in any form, whether it be games, mediums, or horoscopes.

Now about believing in ghosts.

As recently as 1999, a Gallup poll shows three times as many people said they believe in ghosts as those polled in 1970.

In the 2000s a popular TV series explores the world's most haunted places. Ghost hunters have their own "reality" show. Weekly dramas involve themes such as mediums who supposedly contact the dead.

The world of the paranormal has become quite popular in movies, books, and all forms of entertainment. The question is why?

Some say it's because the world of science dominated thought trends during the 1950s, 60s and even into the 1970s. People had great optimism. They believed scientific research would eventually cure all ills, conquer space, and offer solutions for most every kind of problem.

While it's true the world of technology has rapidly outgrown our ability to keep up (my computer is out of date before I carry it out the door of the store) science has failed to fulfill these expectations.

What's left? The pendulum swings from scientific reason—what can be measured, touched, weighed, caused to react in a chemically predictable manner—to that which cannot.

An unhealthy fascination with the occult appears to be growing.

This book is not written with that view in mind. It is simply a collection of my father's observations, many of them humorous, and his ghost stories are meant only for family fun. What he has learned for himself over the course of his life is evident as the stories progress.

Any churchgoer will be pleased.

Editor's note: Many men have written well, but Jones has written **weller.** (Yes that's a word simply because I made it up. That's called poetic license.)

I can say that because I'm his biggest fan. The following verse he wrote while watching a small child comforting her smaller sister. It's one of my favorites.

Did You Ever?

Did you ever see a little kid helping a smaller child to
cross a street?
Or some graying senior attending one even older and
more weak?

Some youth with strong, commanding, vibrant personality, tending one who is far less endowed, making
him feel an equal with the crowd?

Ever notice the path such people trod?
They seem to walk a little closer, even hand in hand
with God.

"Keep away from people who try to belittle your ambitions. Small people always do that, but the really great make you feel that you, too, can become great." Mark Twain

Halloween Adventure

There is a darkly shaded area along a stretch of deep water in Sans Bois Creek where wolves love to congregate and howl a lonesome cry on cold, snowy nights when the moon is full.

Farm dogs shiver and curl up tightly inside their sheds, or whine and scratch at the door, begging entrance. Children pull covers over their heads. Grownups snuggle deeper in their beds and wrap their quilts more tightly about themselves as night winds whisper at their windows.

During cool, clear October nights, the moon casts its rays through the brown, dead leaves of autumn, lighting ripples on the black waters of Sans Bois Creek.

In the small Oklahoma community known as Kinta, youth who are seeking Halloween thrills sometimes dare each other to walk into the deep, tangled mass of vine-wrapped trees and through the dark shadows haunting the bank of Sans Bois Creek's Wolf Pool. It's a thrilling test of bravery. The kids have a choice—a walk by the Wolf's Pool, or a venture into the Louisville cemetery at midnight. Most young folks don't go near the cemetery since the time Willy's old coon hound treed the devil there one windy night.

Fifth-graders, Steve and Bobby lived south of Kinta on neighboring farms near Sans Bois Creek. Back then, there were no video games, or even television, so when trick-or-treating was over in the town, the last school teacher's outhouse tipped sideways, and the final popcorn ball eaten, there was little more to do. Maybe that's why during recess at school Steve suggested, "Bobby, you ain't afraid to go with me tonight to the Wolf's Pool are ya?"

Bobby's eyes widened. "You mean on Sans Bois Creek? That's a crazy idea. I'll go any old place that you will. But haven't you heard what old man Simmons told my dad about seeing a big, silver wolf there one Halloween night? He said the thing swam to shore, stood up, and became a hairy-faced man with long, sharp teeth. Simmons said he watched the creature look up at the moon and howl like a wolf before it ran into the woods. The next day a feller was found with his throat torn out. They said the wound must have been from the teeth of a large animal."

"That old story's been around since my grandpap was a kid, but it ain't true," said Steve. "I dare you to come with me tonight. We'll watch the creek water 'cuz it's Halloween. And if there's anything to it, we'll see for ourselves."

The boys agreed to meet at Wolf's Pool at moonrise that night.

Now, it so happens that Cindy Elwood had heard the same story from her daddy, and she asked her best friend, Pammie, to go with her to the pool at moonrise that night. "I want to see if there are any witches, goblins, or wolves congregating there on Halloween," Cindy giggled.

Pammie didn't laugh. Instead she half whispered. "It scares me just to think about being there at night, but I'll go if you will."

"Course I'll go," Cindy declared. "You know as well as I do there's nothing at Wolf's Pool at night that isn't there in the day time. Just trees. Water. Maybe a deer or a rabbit. That's all. I'm not scared. I've been swimming there lots of times. Let's go. It'll be fun. We can say there wasn't any wolf man and have a great story to tell at school on Monday. Everyone will think we're very brave, too."

Feeling like daring adventurers, the two girls planned to meet at Cindy's house that evening and walk to Wolf's Pool in time to see the moon rise.

As the sun went down that Halloween night, each of the four kids regretted agreeing to go and secretly wanted to back out, however they also dreaded being called a chicken. That's about the worst name in the world, and any fifth grader will do most anything to avoid it, including a daredevil walk on the rotting suspension bridge spanning the creek. So that evening, Cindy and Pammie walked down the shady, wooded trail toward the pool.

An owl called softly, "Hooo, hoooo," and the girls froze in sudden fright. Finally Cindy said, "That was just an old hoot owl. They holler like that every night."

The girls shivered with relief and walked on quietly through the snarl of vines and trees all the way to the edge of the bank. They saw nothing. The moon rose slowly above the trees and cast its silvery light upon the dark water, causing an eerie fluorescent glow. The watchers sat down on a log in the shadows and waited, shivering with excitement.

From the other side of the black pool they heard soft, rustling sounds. Something was creeping through the trees. Dry leaves and twigs snapped and voices whispered.

Too scared to run, the girls sat frozen on the log.

"Oh my, I wish we would have stayed home!" whispered Cindy.

"If I ever get home, I'll never back come here again," Pammie agreed, so frightened she could hardly breathe.

The water began to ripple and make waves. A dark shape broke the surface just as the moon peeked through the branches and shone full upon the creek. Across the pool, two shadowy figures stood motionless, gazing at the strange object rising from the water.

"What—what is that across the pool?" whispered Pammie.

"Shhh!" Cindy held a finger to her lips. "Looks like two goblins."

"But they aren't as tall as goblins should be,"said Pammie.

Breaking the water's shiny surface, the ears, nose and finally the head of a large silver wolf took shape. It swam to shore, climbed out, pointed its snout towards the moon, and howled a long, mournful cry into the night before darting into the woods.

The shadows across the pool took the shape of two boys who began to run for the roadway on the far side of the trees. Cindy and Pammie took flight as well. As they splashed across the nearby shallow ford, Cindy exclaimed, "Pam? Those two goblins looked an awful lot like Steve and Bobby."

"That's just what I was thinking," said Pammie, catching her breath.

When they reached the white ribbon of road in the moonlight, sure enough, Steve and Bobby appeared at the same time. The kids recognized one another and slowed to a walk. Then they started to laugh, giddy with relief and a sense of security, now that they numbered four.

Cindy said, "I'll tell you what. Let's all go to my house for treats. I've seen all the tricks I care to see for one night!"

Pammie exclaimed, "You boys sure scared us! We thought you were goblins."

Steve replied, "Holy mackerel! We thought you two were goblins!" They all laughed. Then Bobby said, "But one thing I want to know. How in the world did you get that dog to swim to the top of the water like that? What a trick!"

"We—" the girls stammered together, "we didn't have a thing to do with training any dog! What was that awful thing?"

"You didn't train it?" Steve said in disbelief. "Then who did?"

The foursome grew quiet and started to hurry toward Cindy's home. As they walked, they heard a long, mournful wail from somewhere in the woods. An old owl hooted in answer, and a large bat flitted silently across the face of the pale moon.

The kids ran without a backward glance all the way to Cindy's house. They promised each other never to go back to Wolf's Pool on Sans Bois creek again.

It was an adventure they longed to forget, and never did.

(See, I told you I could scare the dickens out of you.)

2

Blame It On Adam
(But Not All of It)

I think we took Shakespeare a little too seriously when he said a rose by another name would smell as sweet. Some names do not bring to mind the fragrance of a flower and, in fact, produce thoughts of the opposite kind of smell (as in whiffing a barnyard). Being identified by the wrong thing can actually damage self image.

Consider the poor female dog called by a name that rhymes with *witch*. I have more respect for the faithful, loving canine than to use such a name. How embarrassing it must be for her. And don't tell me dogs don't understand the language of humanoids. My dog knows dozens of words. Probably more, but he won't admit it. He's too much of a gentleman.

Then there's the burro. This faithful burden-carrier has another not-so-nice name. I once had a burro, and I wouldn't have dared insult the little creature by calling it an ass. Yes, that's his biblical name alright. One ass was smart enough to open its mouth and verbally warn the prophet Balaam not to go through a narrow pass. Tell me he didn't deserve a better name.

When I was a kid, my sisters and I called them Jennys. My little sister's Jenny threw her once, right in the front yard before breakfast. Lucy said she had a little trouble getting over its long ears, but she landed on the grass, same as me.

Calling a burro a Jenny wouldn't set well today. Not if the Jenny happened to be a male donkey. Well maybe it would be alright. After all, we alternate both male and female names for hurricanes in these days of equal rights.

Whoever thought a hurricane would complain?

Now that I think about it, that's all they do actually. Pucker up, blow hard, and sputter. It's different for snow storms. I suppose that's because no snowflake wants to take all the responsibility for a blizzard.

The poor platypus hasn't protested his name, but if I were one I'd probably be marching in Washington. I'd get a listening ear too. Congress is completely against discrimination of all types and encourages us to be more considerate of animal rights. I'm certain that if he had another name, the platypus would have a better self image.

Here's probably what happened. Adam grew tired near quitting time of day and said, "Let's just call it the platypus and let it go at that."

Then there's the sloth. It takes him thirty minutes to climb five feet from one limb to another. When he gets there, he wraps his tail around the limb and just hangs upside down for days. If we called him by another name, perhaps the poor old sloth could hold up his head and feel respected.

The goose is yet another creature in need of a name change. At times, people have used the word *goose* for someone who has done, or said something silly. The goose actually is a highly intelligent creature and takes good care of any other goose which might tire or become wounded during a flight. That's something a humanoid doesn't always do for his fellows.

It's also common to call someone a turkey if he does something silly. "Turkey" might actually be an appropriate term for silly behavior after all. Consider how the bird calls a loud, "gobble, gobble, gobble" to let the sportsman know his exact location on a frosty morning during hunting season. A goose wouldn't do that. We'll leave the turkey with his name indicating silly behavior. It fits.

Now how about that magnificent creature, the horse? When we refer to a dumb-stunt-pulling humanoid as a horse's hind quarters, we don't clarify the humanoid's personality trait so much as we insult the horse.

This mistreatment of beautiful, intelligent animals has got to stop.

I respect animals. I truly do. However I don't know anyone who is too friendly with snakes, mosquitoes or tics. If one of those critters bites me, I think it's perfectly acceptable to show a little irritation. Maybe it's not the Christian thing to do, but neither will I turn the other cheek. If a snake should strike me on the cheek or any place, I can truly say I might actually use language. I can always pray for the snake later after killing it, because after all, it was only doing its thing.

They tell me Adam brought this kind of torment on us, causing us to be subjected to tics, crawling things, poison ivy, stickers and thorns. We have to accept these things without complaining.

I will say this. Since I've been attending the Kinta Baptist Church, I have learned to excuse a tic for biting me. I just say, "Okay, I forgive you, and now I'm on your side. Is there anyone I can help you bite?"

This really doesn't help me feel any better, but it seems to help the tic's feelings. Congress would be proud. We don't want any unhappy tics crawling around.

Oh, by the way, the language I use when a critter stings and bites is a word like "darn" or "shoot." People who use that word, well they probably end up going to a place called Heck. It's only somewhat warm there, not boiling hot like the other place.

On that thought, Christine and I have been attending a revival at Kinta. I'm about religion the same way my kindergarten granddaughter, Danae, was on her first day of school. She walked up to the teacher and spelled C-A-T. She topped that off with R-A-T, and I'm convinced she also spelled the word "philanthropist" as well, but I can't verify it. Then she told the teacher she was ready to go home as she was educated adequately and could dispense with the rest of the school year.

I have that attitude toward religion. I already know the devil is after me, and I already intend to do whatever it takes to avoid him. So why go to every revival in town?

There was a time when I doubted the existence of the devil. Then I supposed that if there were no Hell, a number of good preachers have been earning their wages under false pretenses.

It all started with Adam's big mistake. He was commissioned to name all the living creatures as he saw fit. At that time humanoids did not have Equal Rights Committees to ensure that all animals and insects would feel good about themselves, so Adam didn't give them equally nice names. We have had animals with low self esteem ever since.

I don't want to put all the blame on Adam. The way I see it, every living being, humanoid or other, can surely say thanks to Adam for not calling him a platypus.

School Daze
(The Wald Hyerenna)
"One of the best things in the world is to be a boy; it requires no experience, but needs some practice to be a good one." Charles Warner

I was barely the age of ten when Herbert Hoover was president. The Kinta School District had hired a new superintendent and discipline was strict. A kid could get into trouble at school, or even off the school grounds, before he knew it if some wayward action were reported.

We boys especially had to mind our P's and Q's everywhere we went. I never really knew what my P's and Q's were and would just as soon not mention my P's anyway.

Those were the days when I first noticed there were two times for suffering. When I was doing something wrong and when I was doing something right. Not that I ever deliberately did anything wrong, except pull a few of the girls' pony tails.

Those also were the days when children kept their elbows off the table, sat up straight as they were able, and were told they should be seen and not heard. (I've since decided children also should be seen and not smelled.)

My Aunt Molly was the proprietress of the Kinta hotel— the only hotel *ever* in that great four-block-long metropolis.

In those years, Kinta was actually a thriving community of cotton farmers and cattle ranchers. A railroad ran through the meadow south of town. There was a tall, red-brick bank building which got robbed once. For years afterward, you could see where the outlaws had removed the bricks from an outer wall. Maybe that's why the town installed gas lamps to be lighted on the streets at night. This was a marvelous sight to a country boy who had only seen the dim glow of coal oil lamps in the family farm house. Town was an exciting place.

On the night of the incident, I had been granted the huge pleasure of spending the night with my cousin, Bud Roberts, at the hotel.

Bud and I set out to enjoy the sights and the crowds. We were having a fine time pulling each other in his coaster wagon when he managed to commit the crime of the week. He bumped into a little six-year-old girl's leg. She might have giggled, so slight was the impact, but she preferred to play the role of victim. (I've noticed lots of women do that these days and call themselves women's-lib-something or other.)

Now Bud was the instigator of crimes such as this one, and he was also an expert at appearing innocent. That meant I became the chief suspect, as it was misconstrued that I had been the one guiding the coaster wagon. Actually, we were taking turns pushing each other, and Buddy was steering.

Yes, Bud did intentionally and maliciously steer the wagon into little Dorothy Martindale.

Dorothy's older sister Alma expressed her indignation toward us with great verbal skill. That's when little Dorothy decided to whimper a little to add fuel to the fire.

Alma then ran to her mother who was standing in a line of some thirty people waiting for the Kinta Garage to open its doors. The garage doubled as a theater on Saturday nights at that time and showed mostly B-grade westerns starring Tom Mix (with the high-pitched voice) riding and shooting across the silver screen.

"Momma, Jones ran into Dorothy with a coaster wagon!" Alma tattled.

Before I could explain that I had not been the one steering, Mrs. Martindale hollered, "Jones, you little wald hyerenna!" (That's the way she pronounced the words.)

Her words chilled me to the bone. I was speechless. I couldn't sleep that night, thinking the principal would get wind of the incident, and I'd be in for public humiliation at school. I was no doubt the meanest kid that ever lived. I dreaded each school morning and went around for days pondering what kind of awful thing Mrs. Martindale had called me.

I really thought I was ruined for life. The weight of my fear grew so heavy I couldn't bear it any longer. I had to come clean and confess the whole, awful matter. I waited until Mom was in a cheerful mood. Then hesitantly, I asked, "Momma, what is a wald hyerenna?"

I held my breath, truly afraid for her to discover the shameful truth about me. Could she stand the heartbreak she would suffer at having a son labeled such a thing?

She smiled and said, "Well, a wild hyena is an animal similar to a big, ugly dog, and it lives on the plains of Africa."

Man, that explanation took a load off my mind. I had been certain that something as horrible as a wald hyerenna had to live in the darkest pits of Hades. However, no one could mind looking like a big, ugly dog from Africa.

Mom must have seen the enormous relief on my face, because she burst out with the best laugh I'd heard from her in a long while. It was music to my ears. I knew she didn't mind ugly dogs, because we always had a few hanging around the front porch, and she fed them and talked nicely to them.

Being called such a name had almost caused me to become a psychopath, a criminal, a drug smuggler, and worse.

But an ugly dog? That I could handle. I've never known a dog I didn't like.

One of these days, I'll ask Momma what P's and Q's are. Well the Q's anyway.

Back When

Little Dorothy and Alma Martindale lived with their family at the pump station, a status symbol in those days. They had hot and cold running water, electric lights, and gas for heating comfort in the winter.

When I was a senior in high school, booming Kinta also had a doctor who set up a clinic in an old frame building that had once been the post office. He managed to roundup about a dozen 'volunteers' to come in and have a tonsillectomy for the huge sum of fifteen dollars. I was one of the unwilling few. After he removed my tonsils, the Martindale family took Mom and I to their house to spend the night, so I didn't have to travel all the way out to the farm while in pain.

I was always friends with the Martindale family, even if they did call me a "wald hyerenna."

Born Writer

I am what one might call a born writer. I can make up words to a song at the drop of a hat. They might not make sense, but they will rhyme. I can certainly compose better lyrics than the repetitive "There Goes My Heart Again," by Fats Domino any day.

Remember the song, "How Much is That Doggie in the Window?" It was stolen it from me, although my version was slightly different. I sang it, "How mooch-a little pooch-a in the winder?"

Once I composed an entire theme right off the top of my head in English class. I held a blank sheet of Indian Chief note-book paper in my hand and recited perfectly as if I were reading. I got away with it perfectly too, until the teacher began to compliment me.

The girl, who later became valedictorian of our class, noticed my page was blank and blurted. "Mrs. Malloy, there is not one word written on Jones Barnett's paper!"

Mrs. Malloy said, "Jones, let me see your paper."

I felt like a criminal when I handed it to her, completely embarrassed. Then of all things, she actually gave me another, even greater compliment.

"That was an excellent composition you made up. What could you accomplish if you put forth even half the effort that the others do?"

Mrs. Malloy gave me a "B" grade on my verbal composition, probably much to the chagrin of the tattler.

Perhaps that changed my attitude toward education. I've always heard that a little knowledge is a dangerous thing, but who decides when he knows enough to be out of danger? I didn't want to be in either category.

Books are wiser than the reader until read. I have always enjoyed a good book, and have spent many hours with Mark Twain, Edgar Rice Burroughs, Edgar Allen Poe, Max Brand, Hemingway, Jack London and so many others. A person who reads good literature is self-educated.

Of course much of what passes for literature these days should probably be labeled "gynecology."

My mother had a word for entertainment which she thought improper. She called it "unsanitary." (Actually, the older ladies in my family were very Victorian in their understanding of propriety. They would not even refer to the legs of a table as "legs," and instead called them "limbs.")

The following is my first attempt at poetry. Mrs. Malloy was teaching English literature and we were studying Robert Burns, at the time.

To A Snowflake
Ye wee tiny flying, fluttering flurries
Of almost forgotten days when winds blow
And comes the snow,
I flinch at the thought, almost dazed by the pain,
As I see you melt in the slush and mud,
And it reminds me of worse days
When comes the rain.—Burns Barnett

Kinta's Haunted Hotel

The following mystery happened on a night I spent in town with my cousin, Bud Roberts, at Kinta's only hotel, a large two-story frame building that creaked when the wind blew and creaked when it didn't.

Every time I slept in that rattle-riddled, old building, I heard or saw things that still cause me to wonder. If I woke up during the night, I wondered what caused me to waken. I would lie very still, hardly daring to breathe. I'd hear the distinctive sound of heavy foot steps coming up the rickety stairwell.

Those slow, measured steps would always come to the very top of the stairs, pause a moment, and start down the hall to the very room where my cousin and I were sleeping in our beds. They would approach the door and pause, never seeming to leave. I would lie there smothering under a blanket pulled up over my head. Eventually, I would drift off to sleep again. The next morning I'd wonder if I had dreamed the entire thing.

But there was one night in particular when I know I was wide awake. I woke with a terrible thirst and a very dry mouth. Since I always prided myself on being a kid who could overcome fear, I decided to get out of bed, walk down the hall and get a drink of water.

The moon cast a bright glow through the windows, and diffused light spilled into the hallway. I walked toward the veranda where the water was kept and met a figure wearing a nightdress and a tall, peaked night cap. I had no doubt that the figure was my Aunt Molly, so I simply passed by, got a cool drink of water, and went back to bed.

The next morning at breakfast, I happened to mention, "Aunt Molly, we were both thirsty at the same time last night, weren't we?"

She looked puzzled and asked, "Why do you say that?"

"We met in the hallway when I was going to get a drink," I explained without a second thought.

"Honey, I wasn't up during the night," she said simply.

I let the matter drop, but I've thought about it many times over the years. There were no other guests in the hotel on that particular night.

Who was the figure in the nightdress?

I never found out.

On a different occasion, Bud and I, both around fourteen years of age, had been to a party and were returning to Aunt Molly's place. We slipped inside as quietly as possible because it was very late. I was asleep almost as soon as my head hit the pillow.

Sometime later I heard the wind picking up, moaning and shuffling about the window like an anxious beast pawing to come inside.

The window curtains were blowing straight out across my bed. The room was black as pitch. No moon, no stars, and no light from the gas lamps, now extinguished, on the street below. A bright flash lit up the room and a clap of thunder rattled every board in the building.

I have always enjoyed a good thunderstorm if it's not too severe. A storm relieves the heat of a summer night, so I snuggled under the sheet anticipating a good sleep.

Another crash of thunder. Another flash of lightning. The wind began to whip torrents against the building and through the open window. I got up to close it before my bed got soaked.

That's when I saw it—a shadowy figure standing in the downpour on the walk facing the entrance to the hotel. I couldn't take my eyes off the tall, rain soaked form and finally had to wake Bud, which was no easy task.

He eventually managed to shake himself out of restful slumber, muttering, "What is it, Jones?"

I pointed to the window.

He looked.

Then he turned to me. "Did you see something standing there at the door?"

"I sure did," I whispered.

"What in the world?"

"I don't know."

I looked out once again. The figure had vanished. That's when we both distinctly heard the sound of the front door opening, heavy footsteps entering the lobby, and starting up the stairs. The mysterious intruder reached the second floor and marched steadily down the long corridor toward our door.

I waited, tense with fear of the unknown; however the tension wasn't as bad as on previous occasions, since I had Bud with me to share the suspense this time. We sat there in the dark waiting for something—we knew not what.

Bud finally lighted a cigarette, and I whispered, "Light one for me too." That was the first time I ever smoked, and I lived to regret it, but of course no one knew back then that tobacco would eventually kill us.

We smoked three cigarettes sitting there in the dark room, waiting to find out what might happen next. Finally the footsteps moved away from our door and receded down the hall.

When it seemed our visitor had left for the night, we let out deep sighs of relief.

My thoughts turned to mischief. I asked Bud if he had heard the story of the lady in white. It seemed the night was perfect for a spooky tale.

"The lady in white? No, but I guess I'm about to hear it. You know every scary story in the book and then some. Go on. Tell me," said Bud.

"It's about a young woman whose sweetheart was supposed to meet her on a rainy evening," I spoke in a somber, dramatic tone.

"They planned to elope, but a terrible storm blew up. The young man drowned in a raging flood as he tried to swim his horse across Rock Creek. When the lady heard what happened, she ran to the creek at midnight and hurled herself in and drowned."

Bud said, "That's kinda sad, but not too scary."

"No," I added. "Here's the scary part. It's said that every year on the anniversary of his death, a lady in a white gown appears around midnight and plunges into the creek to join her lost love."

Bud sat there in silence.

I rolled over in my bed and soon went back to sleep. My cousin said he couldn't sleep a wink for the remainder of the night, even after the storm blew over, the moon appeared, and the crickets began to chirp again.

He wasn't exactly pleased that I had told him the yarn and then slept while he sat there wide awake in the dark.

Back When

I've always been good at spinning a spooky tale, whether I have heard it before or not.

People are interested in the extraordinary, in tragedies, and mysteries. Nobody wants to hear stories about everyday, ordinary, mundane things. Suppose I told you about a kid who went to school, wrote his theme, made an A, never got into mischief, and never even got called a single bad name. That's about as exciting as watching paint dry.

A lady in white or a mysterious figure will perk up a listener's ears and usually will not put them to sleep from boredom. It worked for Bud.

Reading back over what I have written, I must add the following:

When I say that I wondered about the things in this story, I mostly wonder if I didn't have an overactive imagination.

Wondering

The following "Letter to the Editor" from Jones Bar-nett appeared in the *Tulsa World*:

In remembering the political debate between Lloyd Bensten and Dan Quayle, I wonder how many supporters Mr. Quayle would have gained or lost had he replied to Mr. Bensten's remark, "Sir you certainly are no John Kennedy," by answering simply, "Thank God."

Jones was suddenly famous (or infamous) on eight planets. He made the following remarks:

"Now about being a published writer—everyone respects me, holds me in awe, loving, loathing, fawning over me, and in general causing me to feel important, respected, hated, honored, booed, and some more wonderful things. I will get accustomed to it one day, I hope."

Civil War Soldier
Speaks His Mind
(Civilly or Not)

Growing up in the years when radio was a rarity and movies barely invented yet, the only entertainment we kids had was what we invented ourselves. (I've said that already, but some readers no doubt need to be reminded.)

My grandpa, Marion Barnett, was a Civil War veteran and I always tried to coax him into telling me his experiences. He was not often willing. I learned why after serving in the Army during World War II.

Marion served in the 21st Missouri Infantry under his uncle, Captain Taliaferro. He enlisted as a private, won a battlefield commission, and eventually got promoted to the rank of captain. He served five years, was wounded twice and nearly died from blood poisoning as well as from drinking poisoned water. He eventually came home and raised a family.

Following is an actual event involving Marion Barnett, a copy of a letter about him, written in a flourishing hand on Oct. 8, 1864, and addressed to the Colonel, Headquarters Draft Rendezvous near Benton Barracks, Missouri.

Colonel,
I have the honor to report that on visiting the barracks and Company quarters to see that the lights were out and the Rendezvous quiet and the sentinels at their posts and attentive to their duties, I found lights in the temporary quarters of one of the detachments sent here to be mustered out.

I immediately gave orders for the lights to be extinguished, when someone near the door said, "You have
come to the wrong door."

I replied I had not, and that the lights must be out as it
was after Taps. The same voice near the door replied,
"Go to Hell."

I immediately entered the quarters and attempted to
arrest the man, and said, "I allow no one to use that
kind of language at any time and especially to the "officer of the day."

I caught hold of him when his bedfellow across from
the (cursing) man said, "I will *not* go to the Guard
House."

Just at this time, someone in the quarters said, "We will
have to get up and help." I called for the Corporal of
the Guard, and as I stepped back to the bunk, a man
near where the light was burning said, "I am captain of
this company, and that man is one of my sergeants.

I replied I did not care if he was Lieutenant or Captain, I
did not allow anyone to use such language to me.

As soon as I found out he was a sergeant, I ordered him
under arrest and told him I should report his case to
you this morning.

His name is **Marion Barnett**. I do not know the number of his regiment.

I am very respectfully your Servant,

P. Morrison, Captain V.R. C. and Officer of the Day

Seems to me, Marion had about all he could take. We
kids never heard him say a curse word in his life. His company was awaiting discharge at the time of this incident. I
suppose tired, battle-weary soldiers might be provoked into
using words out of character such as "Go to Hell."

Actually that wasn't as bad a suggestion as it sounds, since the broad way to that place is supposed to be enticing. It's just the end of the road that's not so nice.

Whether or not Marion was arrested by the tattler, I do not know.

A separate interesting bit of Marion's family history shows a little more about his character.

Although he was a sergeant in the Union army, Marion's step father, surnamed Furr, was a Confederate supporter. As you would imagine, this created quite a tension between the two.

Furr was well off and had good horses which he allowed the Confederate soldiers to use, and later he apparently joined up with the Rebels.

The story is that Furr and Marion both arrived home on furlough at the same time. I don't know how two soldiers from enemy armies handled being at the supper table together. One can imagine the atmosphere was somewhat tense.

Marion chose to sleep in the barn that night.

Whether or not he told his step father to go to Hell is unknown.

At least the two men did not attempt to kill each other.

They were after all, civil soldiers.

The following is a blend of fact and fiction (more fiction than fact).

The Mademoiselle

During the late days of September 1917, Luke Baxter received his letter from the military to report for a physical examination. Luke was about 5 ft. 6 in. tall and weighed around 118, but he passed the exam with flying colors. This was a major event in Luke's heretofore uneventful and rather unremarkable life.

He had grown up on his father's forty-acre farm, chopping cotton in the hot sun, harvesting corn in the fall, and driving a team of mules to haul supplies. Luke's mom always had a meal—sometimes home-cured ham, corn bread, beans and fresh garden vegetables—on the table every evening promptly at six.

The nearest town was six miles over the hills and through the woods, so Luke didn't get there very often except for school days. He had heard stories about the movie theater in Sapulpa, but that was a farther distance. A good book was something to be treasured. He found adventure in the pages of books.

Sometimes a neighbor would host a party and Luke would go, however he was shy and the girls all seemed interested in other guys. He liked to join in the singing that accompanied some of the games—great lyrics such as, "Happy was the miller boy that lived by the mill, the mill turned around with a free good will."

He also went through the motions and sang the words to the "Hokey Pokey" with the kids. At times, he doubted that's what it's all about, but who knew? The melodies stayed in Luke's mind, and he would hum all the way home after the gatherings.

Now Luke's country actually needed him. Ma and Pa were happy to see him so pleased, but Ma hugged him with a fierceness he had not experienced before.

On the morning of his departure, Luke had to feed the mules and milk two cows before leaving for Sapulpa. He finished the chores and headed for the house, glancing over his shoulder and seeing the old mule looking toward him, long ears extended. The words of a tune sprang to his lips. "Goodbye Ma, goodbye Pa, goodbye mule with your old hee haw."

Pa Baxter looked away and brushed a gnarled hand across his eyes. "Luke, that old mule is going to pick those long ears way up when you come walking out to the barn again some day."

With basic training soon finished, Luke was sent to Fort Sam Houston where he sat with a company of green soldiers and enjoyed entertainment by a troop from Houston. He quickly picked up the lyrics: "K-k-k, Katie, beautiful Katie, you're the only g-g-g girl that I adore. When the ma-moon shines, over the mountain, I'll be waiting at the k-k-k kitchen door."

He grinned, supposing the song writer must have been a stutterer. The songs brought to mind the old cow shed, the barn lot, and the farmhouse with its lamp light in the window where Ma and Pa were waiting for him. Luke wondered if the other guys had a beautiful girl waiting back home for them—someone besides an old mule. He wished he had attended more of the neighbors' parties and been a bit more sociable to the girls. "But shucks," he told himself, "I haven't been many places. I'll know how to act more social when I get home."

The Grand Finale of the show promised to be a huge hit. Luke had never heard such singing with so much stirring optimism. "Goodbye Broadway, hello France, we're ten thousand strong. Goodbye sweethearts, mothers, wives; It won't take us long. Goodbye Broadway, hello France; Now it's you we're fighting for; so goodbye Broadway, hello France; we're going to help you win this war."

Not one soldier of the entire company, their hearts fired by the rousing chorus, would have shrunk from tackling the whole German Amy single handedly.

After the wild cheers and applause, a handsome Dough Boy walked out on stage. His uniform fit to perfection and his leather leggings couldn't have been more perfect. Luke was suddenly aware his own uniform didn't fit so well, but then his legs were skinny. He told himself, "I'm going to fill out now that I've been in training and eating all this good army food."

At that moment a picture of the prettiest girl he had ever seen flashed on a screen, and the troops started singing, "The Mademoiselle from Armenteers, *parlez-vous*. . . and that perfume behind her ears; hinkey, dinkey, *parlez-vous*."

Luke couldn't keep from laughing out loud. Those were the funniest words he'd ever heard. Were they French? He decided he must learn some of the language as soon as possible.

He also knew in that moment, gazing on the lovely face on the screen, that there was nothing he wouldn't do for the lovely Mademoiselle from Armenteers.

After the show that night, Luke wrote a letter to Ma and Pa. "I'm going to fight to the last if I must to protect that pretty lady from Armenteers," he declared with enthusiastic determination.

Luke's company finally arrived in France after much sea sickness and tasteless hard tack. The trip on the waves was nothing he wanted to write home about.

When the ship reached Le Havre, a French band played as the troops marched down the gang plank. He felt like a hero.

At once he looked across the crowd for the lovely Mademoiselle from Armenteers and couldn't understand why she wouldn't be there at such an important event.

Soon Luke's company was stationed on a battlefront. He inquired of all the other Dough Boys, "Have you seen the Mademoiselle from Armenteers? Do you know where she is?" They only laughed and said, "Well you might see her one day. Keep looking."

Finally, Luke received a pass to go into Paris. He spent the entire twenty four hours asking every person where he might find the lady from Armenteers. The French people smiled and answered politely, "She is here somewhere. Keep looking."

Luke kept looking. He took advantage of every opportunity.

Then came the day—the desperately-hoped-and-prayed-for Armistice Day. On November eleventh at the eleventh hour, the shells stopped falling. A silence of unimaginable relief swept over France.

There would be no more fighting. The war was over.

"Could this be? If I have to go back now, I'll never find her," Luke thought with sudden mixed emotions. He was very glad the fighting had stopped, but still determined to find the lovely mademoiselle whose picture he now carried over his heart.

When the troops assembled and were transported to their points of debarkation, Luke Baxter could not be found.

People met the trains in Sapulpa, gladly greeting their sons, husbands, sweethearts, and brothers, but Ma and Pa Baxter waited in vain.

They met train after train, until the trains stopped bringing Dough Boys back to their Oklahoma homes. No letters came from Luke.

French citizens began talking of an American soldier who walked the roads and also the streets of Paris, carrying a drawing of the likeness of the Mademoiselle.

As the years went by, Ma and Pa became aware of certain nights when the moon rose over the cow shed. A clear tenor voice could be heard singing, "Hello Pa, hello Ma, hello mule with your old hee haw." On these nights, the mule would bray a greeting to an unseen friend.

Hearing this, the farm couple believed their son was still okay, still coming home again some day.

Perhaps he will. Or maybe he will never cease to look for the lovely lady from Armenteers.

And such should be the end of all Dough Boys and G.I.'s—the young boys fresh from the farm—who went, bravely and willingly to fight for the honor of a great country and to die for a cause they never really understood. As far as some of them knew, it was all about the hokey pokey. Or the Mademoiselle from Armenteers.

Perhaps it is easier to give one's life for something surreal and unattainable, an imagined and perfect beauty after all.

3

A Jeep Or A Peep?

When I was drafted into the U.S. Army in April of 1941, I arrived at Fort Leonard Wood Missouri, and the first thing I saw was a peculiar little vehicle coming toward me. No top, no windshield, and no apparent purpose that I could see except the pleasure of the driver behind the wheel.

"What the heck is it?" A fellow asked. Like most of us, he was from "down on the farm" where supplies got hauled in mule-drawn wagons.

"It's something the Army designed for second lieutenants to play with. Darn! Don't you wish you had one?" Another boy exclaimed.

"Say, when we've done our year's service, wonder if we could buy one?" I asked.

We had been conscripted for a year's military service and were already looking forward to the day of our discharge.

Another draftee said, "That's a Jeep."

A Jeep. So that's what they called it. When I had been in the CCC Camp, there was a fellow assigned to my detail to assist us. This assistant was called a "Jeep."

Now at that time, the word "Jeep" was taken from an old Popeye cartoon episode which ran during the summer of 1937. There was a little animal in the cartoon, about the size of a small dog, and Popeye called it a Jeep. I assumed the vehicle took its name from the cartoon critter.

However, in September of 1941, The *Saturday Evening Post* magazine ran a photo cover of a second lieutenant pointing to a Jeep. Buck privates were instructed to call it a "Command Car." The photo cut lines stated, "This is not a Jeep; this is not a Peep."

Now years later, I've been having nightmares over this conflict of information. It has caused me all kinds of sleepless nights and complexes. I've never wanted to refer to any vehicle as a Jeep, if the Army wanted it properly termed something else, since I was strictly G.I.

I challenge anyone to look up the *Saturday Evening Post* for the September of 1941, or maybe August or October, and see if I remember the photo correctly.

If I'm right, I'm going to sue the government for all the headaches I've had over this misunderstanding.

Best of The Worst

"The worst enemy is the friend who knows where to strike." Anonymous

The tragedy of war is that it uses man's best to do man's worst, and by doing so, turns him into something less.

Somebody else probably said that, but I thought of it first.

War is the most inhuman thing. And yet, there are examples of humanity at its best, even during the worst of times.

I have to begin by saying this actual incident I'm about to relate is surprising to many veterans. It happened to a friend of mine during the German Army break in the winter of 1944, somewhere near Belgium.

Ed was a sergeant in a tank company advancing toward the German troops. His commander ordered them to move forward to the top of a railroad overpass.

"Sir, if we pull up there, we'll draw enemy fire," Ed answered.

The order stood, so the Sherman tank driver obediently rolled ahead facing a certain strike. As soon as it reached the top of the embankment, it took a direct hit. The tank's interior erupted in flames. Ed raised the turret and climbed out, knowing death was imminent, one way or the other.

At once a German bullet struck him. He rolled down the embankment and lay crumpled on the ground. Bleeding and faint, he glanced up to see a German soldier standing over him with a rifle.

"Well, go ahead and shoot me," he said in a voice filled with tired resignation, "I'm going to die anyway."

Blood spurted from his leg.

The German answered, "We don't want to kill you, soldier. We're taking you to the hospital to try and save you."

And that is what they did.

When Ed was well enough to travel, to his further surprise, he was released to return to his own company.

I was hesitant to believe this story, but I know Ed too well to doubt its veracity. He still makes frequent visits to the Veteran's Hospital where the doctors want to amputate one of his legs. He will not consent and walks with a noticeable limp.

For some unknown reason, most people don't want to hear this kind of story from a returning veteran. They'd rather hear a soldier say he shot the German s.o.b.

G.I.s and Dough Boys

"Children play at being soldiers. There is also a time when soldiers should play at being children. May they never forget how." Anonymous

During World War I, soldiers were called Dough Boys. My mother, Josie Adkins, was a young lady during this war, and she said our boys got the name when they entered the fight against the Central Powers. Those troops bragged there was nothing to fear from U.S. soldiers, because we were just a bunch of soft "Dough Boys."

During World War II, our soldiers were called G.I.s. I believe I know where that term came from. Readers may not give a durn, but it's a little bit of history. Who knows? It may win you a game-show prize some day.

Franklin Roosevelt introduced the Works Progress Administration to help the nation get on its feet during the Great Depression.

Old Mrs. Tidwell used to say, "Why'd the depression have to hit when times were already so tough?"

It did hit Okies especially hard, but instead of government handouts, men were given jobs working on streets, roads, building schools, and other government projects like the public park buildings at Lake Carlton. They could hold up their heads, knowing they had earned their wages. (This is the best cure for any kind of depression I know of.)

Younger guys could enlist in the Civilian Conservation Corps (CCC camps). The camps were about the size of a regular Army company of 180 to 200 men and were run in military style.

Discipline was as rigid as the Army's, and the pay was about the same. The camp commander was always a man with a captain's rating in the regular Army.

The camp's work force was governed by the State Conservation Service, engineers, agronomists, and conservation specialists.

I never heard one CCC fellow complain that he didn't enjoy his time in the camps. Classes were held daily in conservation measures, talking radio codes, bookkeeping, drafting, barbering, and many other subjects.

We played baseball, basketball, had boxing tournaments and enjoyed free movies once a week. The food was excellent, and any fellow who entered was a better fellow when discharged at the end of his enlistment.

CCC camps were a darn sight better than any assistance offered presently that I know of. Today's youth are so highly entertained they don't know what it is to pick up a shovel or load rocks on a truck. (I finally got that said.)

Now, back to the term G.I. When you applied for admission to the CCC camp through the local Welfare Department, you were notified to report to the county seat, mine being Stigler. When you got there, you and ten or fifteen others were herded around awhile (Army style) and finally directed to a truck. The truck took you to your destination, and you were processed into camp. Some went to Arizona, California, Colorado and a few other places.

(I'm getting to it now.)

When you finally arrived, the first thing you had to do was strip, shower, and get in line for your issue of clothing and supplies such as soap, shaving cream, toothpaste, and a razor.

You walked down a line and the supply sergeant would throw you a pair of white boxer shorts. As he issued items, he would call out in a loud, forceful voice, and an assistant would mark them off on a note pad. Here's the way it went.

"Three pairs of shorts. G. I. (which stood for government issue.) Three pairs of socks. G.I. Two pairs of shoes. G.I."

The G.I. list included fatigues, dress uniforms, hat, rain coat, overcoat, neck tie for dress and for standing retreat, pillow, blankets and sheet—all G. I.

After receiving the above, you stood in line for small pox, typhoid, and tetanus shots. You could draw a canteen book with enough checks to buy Bull Durham until pay day.

Once an enlisted CCC camp member, you were considered a G.I. and you were made ready for the Army.

Here in Haskell County, I know for certain some of the finest, most loyal men in the land were G.I.s who spent time in the CCC camps. They had nothing, asked for nothing, and gave their all.

Many died quickly in the first battles of the war. Those veterans who survived gave a lot for this land.

What did Kennedy mean when he said: "Ask not what my country can do for me, but rather ask what can I do for my country?"

Ask any G. I. what he did. What did he do for America while working through the Great Depression, learning in a CCC camp, reporting to fight a war? No questions asked, no draft-card burning, and no fleeing to Canada.

I agree that people shouldn't ask what the feds can give them and just sit around waiting for government handouts. On the other hand, when in the history of the world has a nation reached out such a willing hand to other nations in need?

Perhaps that's because we always had G.I.s who were ready and willing to give their all for this country.

**"The law is so concerned with equal rights that if Moses handed down the Ten Commandments today, they would be challenged in court as discriminatory."
Anonymous**

Downright Silly

What makes us discontented with our condition is the absurdly exaggerated idea that everyone is enjoying a life of ease and happiness, and we didn't get our share.

To remedy this awful inequality, our great society honors the act of blaming others, seeing this as a sign of virtue and generosity. I read every day how the government wants to make it up to certain groups for the way they were treated in the past. Anti-discrimination laws are becoming downright silly.

How in the world can the government make it up to anyone for the way a father or grandfather was treated?

I served in the Army during World War II along with about 11,000,000 others. If you interviewed any of these guys, they would find plenty to complain about.

I had K.P. duty when the St. Louis Browns happened to be playing the World Series, and I was discriminated against. I had to keep washing pots and pans while the Browns were throwing the ball. That still causes me consternation, all these years later!

How does the government make it up to the sailors who served in the Navy? Did you ever read *White Jacket* by Herman Melville? Or *Two Years Before the Mast?* Those books literally caused the articles of war to be rewritten after the public read how sailors were flogged, brutally mistreated, half starved, and stripped of every ounce of human dignity.

How much restitution was restored to them? Did they just happen to be living at a time when it was accepted that authorities abused their underlings?

Believe me, the Black people of yesteryear were not the only ones to suffer discrimination. How do you make it up to the soldiers captured and interred at the infamous Andersonville? Starved, fed slop, many died quickly and were lucky to do that. Who can repay these fellows? They were not the ones who started the war.

John F. Kennedy himself admitted there is always inequity in life when he said: "Some men are killed in war, and some are wounded, and some are stationed in the Antarctic, and some in Hawaii. It's very hard in military or personal life to assure complete equality."

My point is simply this. When a government starts to repay for past mistreatment of people, where is it going to stop?

History is a sad reminder there is . . .

Always Another Battle
(The shell that didn't explode)

The lesson in the incident I'm about to describe is the fundamental lesson of all life's battles. That even the most carefully prepared plans can go wrong, and that a seemingly lucky break can make all the difference.

Growing up in the early 1900s, I always romanticized World War I. If I found out a fellow was a veteran of that war, I made it a point to talk to him. Veterans became my heroes as a youngster, probably because I was born during the height of that war, and their stories fascinated me.

World War I veterans thought they had fought the war to end all wars.

Actually, no war ever settled anything.

There's always another battle to fight, no matter how many peace treaties and agreements are signed. Just look at the world around us.

I know too much about World War II, having served in the U.S. Army, where I discovered that I hate war. It ruins good conversation, unless one polishes the story a little.

Some soldiers weren't brave enough to be cowards. I freely admit there were times I was literally shaking from fear of a bomb exploding near me.

Once a shell from a German cannon was fired in my direction. I heard the *whisssssshhhhh* of the trajectory over my head and the thud as it hit the ground about twenty feet from where I lay flat on my belly.

I waited for the shell to explode, literally trembling all over, but not moving otherwise. What was the use?

I survived because that shell was a dud.

Many shells fired by the Germans were faulty, but I didn't know that at the time.

The Sergeant of the Guard relieved me from my post a few minutes later, and I informed him of the shell that had not exploded. He wisely decided to move our guard post at once to another location some three hundred feet away and ordered us to dig in.

The next day I discovered every muscle in my body was completely sore. The soreness was from the tension of the moment I spent waiting for the bomb to explode.

Every soldier also knows what it means to get fox-hole religion. Those promises of dedication may actually impress God in an emergency, but I suspect such religion is not the real thing.

Charles Colton was mostly right when he said, "Men will wrangle for religion; write for it; fight for it; die for it; anything but live for it."

Of course, many guys died in fox holes. They didn't get the chance to live out their promises to God.

The writer of *Ecclesiastes* said time and chance happen to all men. Sometimes a guy gets the chance for a little more time.

I'm grateful I did.

Editor's note: A lucky break? There were those people who never ceased to pray for the safety of their men. Jones was waiting to go ashore at Normandy on D-Day when a violent storm broke. Rough waters kept his ship at sea for a period of two more days after the first wave of troops had landed. By the time his company finally was shuttled to shore, the beachheads were littered with dead bodies. On the night before the storm at sea, Jones' future wife Christine, then a student at Oklahoma Baptist University, felt a strong compulsion to pray for his safety and did so. She has no doubt the Lord answered that prayer.

**"How welcome do bad music and bad reasons
sound when we march against an enemy."
Nietzsche
"How lovely is the song of peace, no matter who
the singer."- Anonymous**

The era of Word War II had a music all its own and many of its popular songs are still played today. Others are long forgotten.

A soldier sings of the girl back home. *K-K-K Katie*, *Over There* (Cause the Yanks are coming and it won't be over till we're over, over there), *Goodbye Broadway, Hello France, To Each His Own, Till Then, The White Cliffs of Dover, Comin' In On A Wing and a Prayer.*

These songs usually bring a sad smile to those who lived through the era. It was said that we American boys actually sang ourselves all the way through and finally out of the war. I suppose we did. We marched, singing: "Ya hadda good home but you left, you're right. Sound off, one, two, sound off, three, four, cadence count. . ."

We sang when tired, when lonesome, or when glad. We sang to forget a dirty, rotten, awful, and inhuman war.

Strange how we have a way of blotting out the bad things from our memories and recalling and even romanticizing the good things.

Let's take this story for instance.

Song In The Night

It was Christmas Eve, 1917, somewhere on the western front. Not much shooting going on. No attack ordered. Each side was hunkered down in the trenches and not one soldier had a desire to go over the top.

Oh, they were well-disciplined troops alright, awaiting orders. They would not shirk their duty. They were ready to charge when the command came. Ready to face machine gun fire and to return it.

What were the Jerries thinking in their trenches on this holy night? What were the Dough Boys' thoughts? Home? A wife or a girlfriend? A table laden with turkey and trimmings? A hope of living to celebrate another Christmas with family?

All were boy soldiers on both sides—boys become men before their time, all lonesome for home and loved ones.

During the quiet calm of the chill winter night in France, a perfectly pitched tenor voice broke the silence. A German soldier singing the well-known hymn, *Silent night*. He actually stepped up out of the fox hole onto No-Man's Land in plain view of all the troops. Somewhere a lone shell burst, lighting the night sky and making the singer even more visible.

Who would have drawn a bead on that soldier, singing so sweetly about a savior born to bring heavenly peace?

Now to top this off (and it's a true story) the Americans and Germans climbed out of their fox holes and actually ap-proached one another. They exchanged gifts of cigarettes, chocolate bars, and other items.

The next day they killed one another, but for that brief moment, they celebrated a gun-silent night as brothers meeting in peace.

Heavenly peace.

That's the only treaty that will finally one day eliminate all battles, all wars, for all time.

Until then, there will always be another battle to fight. Another song to sing.

The Phantom Aviator

Another of my favorite World War II stories is about a Phantom Aviator. That's what we called him back then.

I qualified as an aviator but did not get my birth certificate through the mail in time to be processed, something I always regretted.

Every soldier likes to think there is some kind of benevolent force protecting him in battle. Perhaps that's where the story arose, but it was told as truth.

Various pilots began reporting a phantom flyer who would appear and disappear during their missions and operations. Soon they all talked of seeing him during dog fights (that's what they called it when fighter pilots were shooting one another out of the sky).

They said the Phantom Aviator had long blond hair streaming out behind him through the cockpit. It was actually never known whether he flew a German or an American plane. Maybe neither one.

The way I heard it, an American pilot was in serious trouble, lost, disoriented, and wounded from enemy fire. He managed to keep the nose of his plane up in the clouds, but the fuel was leaking badly, and he knew he would soon crash if he did not find his landing field.

That's when the Phantom's plane appeared through the smoke, and the blond pilot signaled the flyer to follow. The American couldn't tell if it was a German fighter plane and feared being led to enemy territory, but he decided to risk it. He followed his mysterious guide.

Soon he broke through the clouds, recognized his field, and managed to land the crippled plane safely on the ground. The Phantom flyer had disappeared.

There are many such stories. They give us a glimpse of hope in intervention from above. And since I have decided to believe in angels, perhaps the Phantom was of that rank.

Heb. 1:14: "Are they (angels) not all ministering spirits, sent forth to minister for them who shall be heirs of salvation?"

4

Kinta Folks

About five miles southwest of the Haskell County community known as Kinta, you will find a narrow valley between Sans Bois Creek and the Sans Bois mountain range. The farm houses of some of the earliest settlers to the Sooner state could be found there.

When I was a boy, farm houses were located about every half mile, sometimes hidden by the pines, oak, hickory, and elm groves.

Before Sans Bois Creek turns north, all along the valley running east and west for a distance of seven miles is a large area of flat land known as Cooper's Bend. Fewer people settled in the valley west of Cooper's Bend, but some of the families there had children who hiked three miles up the mountain every day to the old Tucker Knob School House. The abandoned building was still standing during my children's youth. My nieces, Nancy, Jodi, and my kids, Harriett and Scott, used to play on the stage there. They even banged on the keyboard of an abandoned piano and used the dusty stage to put on make-believe programs.

While the school was still in use, farm boys grew up hunting wild game in the area. This was during the height of the depression and game was scarce. Folks had to hunt for meat to supplement their gardens. However, quail hunting was exceptionally good.

These boys often became sharp shooters, quite skilled with their rifles. Their daily walks to school and their frequent hunting trips through wooded hills conditioned them for a stint in military service. Most were drafted to build up the U.S. military forces prior to World War II.

Jobs in Oklahoma were few to none at the time, so young men had little choice but to enter the military. Most did not have the opportunity or the resources to even think about college.

As the early signs of autumn blew in on cooler breezes of late evening, corn stalks turned a deep shade of brown and bales of hay were stacked in the barn. The long, hot days of summer grew shorter and the twilight hours grew longer. The first full moon of September glowed pumpkin orange as it rose over the mountains, turning to a ball of gold on its climb up the darkening canopy of night.

No country boy could rest without twisting and turning about on his bed while gazing up at the stars. I suppose the youth felt the same seasonal changes a wild goose feels prior to its flight south for the coming winter.

After school, the boys used to gather for "bull sessions." They swapped laughs over their plans for the future. Some were drawn by the magical lure of California where they were sure to make their fortunes. Some talked of enlisting in the military, and boasted they would conquer the enemy single-handedly (whoever the enemy was). Mostly they spun tales of their hunting and fishing adventures, the sum of their brief life experiences at the time.

Barn dances after the harvest season were always popular and I played a merry fiddle tune for these events from time to time.

Some families living near Kinta and the surrounding area in those days were: Monk and Lilly Mizell, who served great hamburgers to everybody for miles around at their mom-and-pop diner; the Arthur Aldridge family; the Ellington family (no relation to Duke); the Barnett Sartwell family; the Charlie Snow family; the Domey Boggs family; and the Ed Watson family whose son is part of the following strange-but-true event.

This mystery probably has an explanation, but nobody has ever been able to come up with one.

Read on and solve it if you can.

The Mysterious
Spot Light

Contrary to what the reader might think, the valley around Tucker's Knob Mountain is in no way steeped in myths or unusual legends, even though in years long passed Tucker's Knob Mountain had supposedly been the scene of a public hanging. If that isn't fodder for ghostly tales I don't what is, but I never heard a hint of any "haint," spook, or specter regarding Tucker's Knob.

What I have heard is a mystery, told to me as entirely true.

It was late September in 1936, a damp and muggy evening after one of the country dances. A couple of Kinta boys were walking home and had stopped along the side of the road to experiment with smoking a Bull Durham cigarette. At that time, nobody knew that tobacco could eventually destroy your lungs, so most boys smoked, thinking it a harmless pleasure.

Seated comfortably on a rock, their cigarettes glowing red in the dark, the youths were enjoying the stillness of the night. They were totally unprepared for what followed.

Without warning, a blinding light shined down around them and hovered motionless and silent above their heads. They sat spellbound, paralyzed by fright, not knowing what to expect, until the light vanished as suddenly as it had appeared.

Where had it come from? Where did it go?

The mystified boys hurried to their homes, barely able to wait till morning to describe the startling spot light to their parents. Their separate stories were met with silent stares.

People living in the area at the time were realists. They knew that if it rained too heavy at the wrong time, the creek overflowed and ruined the crops. It if didn't rain at the right time, the crops withered and the cattle starved. They also figured that if a pair of country boys said a spot light came from nowhere and shined down on their heads, it had to be imagination, pure and simple—nothing more.

There are those who exaggerate so greatly they cannot tell the truth without lying, however when the boys told me about their unusual experience, I could see by the look in their eyes that something had surely happened.

They took me to the exact spot where the mystery light had appeared, took a stick, and drew a ring of about ten feet in circumference, claiming it approximated the ground covered by the light's eerie glow.

I stood in the center of the circle and looked up. An overhanging hickory limb protruded into the circle. Its leaves looked strangely withered. I did not point this out at the time, but each day I passed by the place, the leaves grew more shriveled on that particular branch. Finally they turned black and fell off.

What had happened to those leaves? To those boys?

They were not affected health wise, however in less than a year, both of them lost their hair.

I eventually forgot all about this strange story during the next forty years or so while I was surveying, raising my family, and cattle ranching.

It was 1976 when I heard the story again, this time from three adult men. They said they were standing together in a spot which I knew to be within a thousand feet of the exact place where the mysterious light first appeared. All three told of a bright light shooting down from the night sky and holding a silent position over their heads for about three minutes.

Those three credible citizens will swear to the truth of this story even today. One of them is a banker, one an engineer, and I do not know the third man's occupation. I also do not know if any of them lost their hair. (And if any of them do wear a hairpiece, I don't know it and wouldn't tell it if I did.)

A puzzle. A mystery.

We live in the days when people often talk of seeing UFOs. I myself have watched mysterious lights floating above the mountains on summer nights. I supposed they were the products of Russian and American space satellites and experimental craft.

There is an explanation. I am a realist in spite of all my spooky yarns.

What Is Sanity?

G.K. Chesterton said, "The man who cannot believe his senses, and the man who cannot believe anything else, are both insane."

What, after all, is the definition of insanity? I have one, but I'm not going to say what it is. Not yet.

It doesn't describe me though, because I have a perfectly reasonable explanation for every stupid thing I've ever done. I am also honest enough to admit all four of my shortcomings. All fourteen. Okay, all forty of them.

That surely makes me a man of reason with my sanity still intact.

Here's what will drive a guy wacko. As reasonable and scientific-minded as I am, I still have no explanation for the mysterious spot light, the night figure in the hotel's hallway, or the stranger in the snow storm.

A Kinta Song

I came upon an article about a place the writer described as "plain as Indiana."

I had never visited Indiana, but I thought surely it couldn't be as plain as all that. I've heard the song about the Wabash and have always imagined Indiana a place of beauty, so I decided I wouldn't stand idly by and let the state be described as blah and humdrum. The Hoosiers surely wouldn't allow such blatant discrimination. (There's that red-flag word again, so hated by the government).

How does Indiana compare to the Sooner State? As a native of Oklahoma, I can describe our wonderful scenery, especially in the mountains, hills, forests, and lakes. Motorists enjoy the Talimena Drive across the Ouachita National Forest, especially in the autumn when the leaves are burnished gold and red. The Kiamichi, Arbuckle and Sans Bois ranges are a mass of greenery in spring with many clear, tumbling springs. Fishing is excellent.

Anyone who remembers the 1930s depression years can recall the best-selling novel about Okies of that era in *The Grapes of Wrath*, by John Steinbeck. The book plainly shows what it meant to struggle for survival in the Dust Bowl. A native of Indiana wouldn't have been caught near an Okie at that time. Merle Haggard's words, "I'm proud to be an Okie from Muskogee," could not have been written then.

When Oklahoma's great football teams were playing at UCLA, they had to hear the pep team singing, "The Dirty, Dirty Okie." I do not believe this song is around anymore, but at that time Okies were considered "not much," a term for almost worthless.

I have to imagine Indiana, where the moon shines on the river and "from the fields there comes the breath of new mown hay. Through the sycamores the candle light is gleaming . . . on the banks of the Wabash far away."

It's a lovely picture the song portrays. So you see what a song can do for a country, a state, or any place. Look what Rodgers and Hammerstein did for Oklahoma. They finally put our state on the map in a far better light than Steinbeck's *Grapes of Wrath*.

It was a wise man who said the country's musicians and writers do more to shape its morality than any other thing.

I intend to put Kinta on the map in a far better way than it has been before and lift the town's morale. Perhaps I'll write a song.

K-K-K Kinta, beautiful Kinta.

No? How about Kinta on my mind?

Or, I left my heart in San Fran Kinta.

I think all the above have already been done. I'll keep working on it.

By the way, I know a guy who went to San Francisco. He didn't see any heart lying around.

Bodie's Civil War
Ghost Story

Bodie Morgan lived with his grandparents in Missouri. Bodie's grandpa was a rarity in those days of 1934.

This old gentleman had a handlebar mustache and a long white beard covering the lower half of his face. He was a Civil War veteran. His sword, complete with saber cuts and nicks on the guard hilt, hung over the mantle along with a copy of his orders to report to Captain Jim Taliaferro, Commander of Company B, Twenty-First Division Missouri Infantry.

Bodie loved to brag about his grandpa's exploits and made up all kinds of tales about battles the old man had won single handedly.

The story I'm about to relate was told by Bodie's grandpa and related to me by my own grandfather, also a veteran of the Civil War.

On a certain Halloween, 13-year-old Bodie came home from school and went straight to tell his grandfather about his planned adventures for trick-or-treat night.

"We're going to scare some folks and play some tricks tonight, Grandpa. The leaves are such a wonderful fall color right now, and the moon is going to be full. If there were such things as spirits, this would be the perfect night for them, don't you think?"

The old man just nodded and made no comment.

"Grandpa, I know you were in the war and many times you had to be surrounded by dead soldiers. It does seem that if there were such things as spirits, you would have seen them. Do you think you ever saw a real ghost?"

Grandpa put some tobacco in his pipe and lit it. He turned his blind eyes toward Bodie. Like my grandfather Marion Barnett, this old veteran had been blind for a number of years.

"Son, I've never told this to anyone, because I never wanted another person in the world to know it. No other person would believe it. I'm the only one who knows it to be true. I could never bring myself to tell my own mother about it, and at times I'm truly sorry for that."

He took a draw on his pipe, puffed out the wisp of blue smoke and sat back.

"Here is the event as I recall. I remember every detail exactly. It was a Halloween night in the autumn of 1862, and my company was bivouacked across the river from enemy soldiers. I was ordered to lead a patrol across the water and scout their exact position. There were four men and myself in a flat-bottomed boat.

"We had to travel as silently as possible, letting our skiff drift gradually with the current, then pull it toward shore. We could see the dying glow of a campfire through the trees, and the moon rays reflecting off a piece of artillery.

"I told the men we'd seen enough, and I wanted to get back across the river. We reached the middle of the waters when old Clint Matthis, always out of step, clumsily tried to move his rifle to keep it from getting splashed by the dripping oars. Sure enough, he dropped the weapon. It struck the side of the skiff and fired. Until that moment the night had been completely still. Now, all heck broke loose.

"Fire erupted from the enemy shore line. We could see flashes from rifles. I never saw a bunch of Johnny Rebs get so upset over an accidental discharge from a rifle. A little thing like that. Guess they were somewhat nervous.

"We bent over our oars and pulled hard toward the willows lining the far shore. I could hear the whirring of the projectiles over our heads. Then there was darkness.

"When I next opened my eyes, I was lying half out of the water near the shore. Rivulets swirled around my shoulders, and I had one powerful headache.

I reached up to touch my hair and my hand came away sticky and warm. I must have slipped in and out of consciousness, because things get hazy at this point.

"When I regained the use of my right arm, I splashed water over my face, but could not muster enough strength to get to my feet. Nauseated, dizzy, and blacking out from moment to moment, I could see the moon through a foggy blue mist. Out of this mist a youthful figure walked toward me. He approached without a word, reached down, took my outstretched hand, and lifted me to my feet with incredible strength. He wrapped an arm around my waist and assisted me back to my company headquarters.

"The next thing I recall is the battalion's doctor tending my head wound, which he said turned out to be only a graze.

"How did you find your way back to camp?" the surgeon asked. "You were completely blind for two days after you got back here."

I lied and claimed I didn't know. Actually I didn't know.

I had assumed one of my fellow soldiers had come to my rescue, but none claimed to have been there. None had seen the youth who supported me on my walk up from the river bank. They said I just stumbled into camp and col-lapsed.

"About two weeks later, I received a letter from my mother. She wrote that my half brother, Critt, a wild sort of kid I truly loved, had run away from home to join me in fight-ing the Rebs. This was all Critt ever talked about, since he had turned fifteen. She wanted me to let her know when Critt arrived and be sure to have my captain send him back home.

"On Halloween night, that year of 1862, Critt somehow stumbled in and reported to the wrong camp—the enemy camp. He was taken prisoner and shot as a spy around the midnight hour. This was the exact time when the youth had appeared in the mist and helped me out of the river.

"I was able to return to duty within a few weeks, and was well enough for several years. A fragment of that missile lodged in my skull and eventually caused me to go blind in my later years."

That's the story Bodie Morgan's grandpa told my grand-pa. I have also heard tales of how Missouri people, living near the area of that bivouac on the river, can hear the sounds of gunfire on Halloween nights over the years.

Editor's note: While the above story was fiction meant to entertain his grandchildren, Jones patterned it after a well-known type of ghostly appearance labeled by research-ers, the "crisis apparition."

Researchers have documented several cases of a dying person's appearances to loved ones. For instance, on March 19, 1917, Captain Eldred Bower, a British aviator was shot down over France. At the exact hour of his death, his niece in England said he appeared to her. Simultaneously, his half-sister in Calcutta also saw his form. Both women said he was briefly visible and then disappeared.

Any ghost story inevitably draws people into a discussion on whether the human spirit survives after death. That belief is universal in every culture since the beginning of time and is accompanied by numerous customs, superstitions, and pagan practices.

For Christians, it's important to note the story of the rich man and the poor beggar Lazarus. After their separate deaths, their spirits were consigned to very different places. The rich man begged to be allowed to return to earth so he could warn his brothers not to "come to this awful place of torment."

He was told by Abraham, "If they do not believe Moses and the prophets, neither will they believe though one should **rise from the dead**." Luke 16: 31.

Clearly, faith in survival of the human spirit is not to be based on ghostly apparitions, but rather on accepting the truth in God's word.

5

Aunt Belle's Tale

My Aunt Belle Barnett's tale is told as historical truth. It involves a Spanish American War veteran who was returning to his Missouri home from serving with Teddy Roosevelt's Rough Riders.

No doubt this guy, I'll call him Hank, was a show off. He was known as a bully. He got off a train in Lebanon, Missouri, loaded with whiskey, loud and boisterous. Several onlookers were hanging around the depot, and maybe he wanted to impress them. Hank pulled his pistol and fired at the feet of some of the Black boys, insisting, "You must take close-order drill at my command."

Nobody appreciated his attitude, and the local police pulled him off the platform.

During the July Fourth celebration, this same fellow took over the dancing platform at the picnic grounds. He made a mistake when he stomped on Charley Barnett's foot. Charley (my father) was only sixteen at the time. He and the bully, well they sort of bumped each other around a little and ended up in a good fight. Neither of them would back off until they winded themselves and simply called it a draw.

Aunt Anna watched the whole thing and wanted to charge at Hank after seeing her brother's nose was bleeding. Later, in a similar incident, Hank undertook to beat up Lon Wright, a Lebanon fellow. The pair rolled on the ground in a clinch. Lon wound up with a fair piece of Hank's ear in his teeth and bit it off.

Guess there was little doubt who won the fight.

As time went on, Lon graduated from medical school and opened a practice. One afternoon, he set out traveling by horse and buggy to make a house call, came upon a wayfarer, and asked the hiker if he wouldn't like to ride a spell.

The fellow gratefully climbed aboard. Soon the doctor noticed he was being scrutinized rather closely by his passenger. Lon glanced at the man and thought something looked familiar about him. The doctor deliberately leaned over to flick a fly from the horse's back, taking the opportunity for a closer look.

"It's the ear on the other side, Doctor Wright," the man stated calmly.

I'd like to think these two fellows shook hands and became friends.

I'd like to think that most folks will take a closer look some day. . .

And also become friends.

Unfinished story

T'was a fortnight ago that I was awakened by a mysterious, late night phone call around 2:30 a.m. The deep male voice said, "Jones, I've got some interesting news for you."

He asked me to meet him at the old canyon house. I don't usually get out of bed and travel at an unknown caller's strange request in the middle of the night, but something in his voice was compelling.

Now let me explain that I had never heard of the canyon house before. Still I somehow knew at once as he mentioned it that I could find my way easily. Something was nagging at my thoughts. I must have been there at least once before, because the path seemed familiar in my mind's eye.

While still on the phone, I seemed to have an odd, dream-like vision. I was just four years old, traveling inside a covered wagon, and we pulled up to a familiar, welcoming farmhouse yard. A very old, bent fellow was talking to the owner, who happened to be my Grandfather. The stooped and bent old man told Grandpa that if he traveled to the top of the second mountain south of the farm and went down to Rock Creek Canyon Trail, he would find an abandoned house. No one had lived there for years at that time.

"What you will experience when you get there will be worth the trouble," the old fellow assured Grandpa.

I wanted to know the caller's name, but he hung up the phone, and I was left to wonder.

What to do? Would anyone in his right mind leave a comfortable house and travel some three miles or more through a dark, misty night at such an hour?

Curiosity. A strange compulsion. I was seized by an intense desire to go and see for myself what this mystery was about. I saddled one of the horses, draped a large rain poncho over myself, and made sure it covered most of the pony as well. Then I headed out, following trails cut through the hills by the drilling companies.

The horse was surefooted and soon plodded to the top of the mountain where a silvery moon peered through heavy clouds from time to time and glanced off the mist, creating an eerie glow.

The canyon trail was visible for a good while, but as I followed it, the timber grew much thicker and darkness closed in like a black cloak.

Soon I could not see my horse's ears ahead of me and had to reach out and touch them to assure myself I was not riding a headless creature.

How could I find an old, abandoned house in this thick darkness? Surely it could not be standing after all this time. My grandpa had been gone for years.

Then I heard a raspy voice speak from nearby. "I see you've made it this far. Get off your horse, and I will lead you inside."

I followed the disembodied voice, somewhat apprehensively, after tying my horse to a branch. I could see dim, ruddy firelight from a cabin window. I followed the guide into the log house, as well-preserved as if it had been built yesterday.

Seated before a burning fireplace, was the same bent, old man I had seen speaking to my grandpa in the dream. "Strange," I remarked. How could this be? In the dream I had been only a child of four and that had been fifty years ago.

The stooped figure studied me carefully with penetrating blue eyes before he spoke.

"I see you have become the man I figured you for when you were just a child. I have been searching for that kind of man a long, long time—someone I could communicate with. You are the one. And now I can explain what must be done."

This story is **"To be continued."**

I now challenge any kid, grandkid, niece, nephew, or their spouses to finish the above tale, as I have some place else to go at this time.

I hope one of them will accept this challenge and complete the story. It will make a great evening's entertainment.

Back Then

I grew up in the days when the old tin well-bucket made a pleasant wind chime on windy nights. The sound was as melodious as any wind chimes purchased in a store, and I liked to hear it. It meant a breeze had arrived.

The family drank cool well water from a wooden bucket. We all used the same dipper, as did the kids at school. And we stayed amazingly healthy, most of the time.

We jumped on hay bales, made swings of grapevines, climbed trees, and swam in the creek.

We had a rain barrel and the water was used for lots of things. It was great for shampooing hair. Older ladies often had blue hair in those days. This was because they used a laundry product called "Bluing" to take the yellow out of their graying locks.

Women boiled water in a black, cast iron kettle for washing the clothes on laundry day.

Bathwater was heated on wood cook stoves, and the kettle of hot water poured into a galvanized tub. Sometimes the entire family used the same bathwater, one at a time of course. Families used homemade lye soap, and it was strong enough to take the hide of a cow at times.

We drank milk fresh from the cow, carried from the barn in tin pails and strained through a cheese cloth. Pasteur would have gasped in horror.

Women knew how to churn butter, and it tasted like butter ought to taste, unless the milk cow had been eating wild onions.

Every farmhouse had a path that led to a little wooden house somewhere out back. Wasps and yellow jackets hung around it in summer, and it was not the most fragrant place in any season.

Everyone tried to avoid going there on cold, frosty nights, but if the trip was required the visitor made it quickly. A Sears wish-book catalogue was kept there. The pages were not for ordering, but they could certainly be perused.

That little house makes me truly appreciate modern conveniences compared to where the family seated themselves back then.

My mother was not a superstitious woman, but once she "cured" my little sister's chicken pox by sitting her outside in the yard and shooing the chickens, causing them to fly over her head.

Mom always laughed about it, and I'm sure she did it more to entertain Naomi than to bring about a cure.

The kids all got dosed with a teaspoonful of coal oil mixed with sugar as a remedy for childhood complaints. I guess it worked because that's how Mom cured me of diphtheria when I was a school boy.

If the creek got out of its banks due to spring rains, we stayed home from school. On one occasion when the creek was high, I tried to make a sailboat out of a tin tub, but it didn't float. I won't say what happened next.

I had an Uncle Jones who grew up on the Barnett farm in Missouri. When he was not yet school age he followed his siblings to school one day after a big rainfall. The Barnett children had to cross the river, south fork of the Osage, to get to school. Their teacher was surprised to see the little boy show up and quickly asked, "Why Jones, however did you get across the river?" He said simply, "I did wide a goat." Nobody ever knew how he really got across.

Hearing of that incident, I can see where I may have inherited my own vivid imagination. I've always been able to answer any question with a story for the amusement of the listener.

I also would have been better off riding a goat across the creek than trying to sail the old tin tub. Where did I get such an idea? Someone must have told me the nursery rhyme, "Rub a dub, dub, three men in a tub." Come to think of it, isn't there something rather odd about three men in tub?

Candy was a rare treat at our house, and I shamefully managed to talk Naomi into giving me most of hers by promising to build her a dollhouse.

I've got to build that dollhouse one of these days.

During long winter evenings when my Mom was in the kitchen preparing supper, we kids were sitting in the other room by the wood-burning heater with the only light being the reflection from the air intake of the stove. This light cast friendly and sometimes strange shadows on the ceiling and made darker corners even darker.

My cousin Rose often showed up at our house to spend the night. She always occupied the piano bench and could beat out some of the best and most popular songs of the day. How she learned them I don't know, because there were no radios in our part of the country then.

People talked with each other in those days, and their kids learned so much, including good listening skills and the art of entertaining conversation.

Now days the TV is blaring and kids are playing electronic games, robbing the family of its bonding time and killing the last remnants of conversation. I think there should be an eleventh commandment—man shall not live by television alone.

I suspect one day I will have to communicate with the younger generation strictly through a handheld device, and I will have to learn an entirely new language.

Each generation has its own vocabulary. I remember once a young motorcyclist walked into Mizell's café and asked. "Where's the sand box?"

"The what?" Lilly blinked at him.

"The sandbox, man, this cat's gotta go."

You see what I mean?

When things get too noisy, going is a good idea. I think I will retire to my office where I can play my fiddle. I'm working on "The Orange Blossom Special," one of my favorites.

Making music is a nice alternative to a blaring television. Too bad more young people don't know that.

It's what you learn AFTER you know everything that counts.

From the days of the tin well-bucket till now, I am still learning.

I have stories yet to tell.

Kinta Kommentator

One of the greatest failures of modern education is that it cannot cure stupidity.

I must comment on the government's decision to give everyone a college education even if it requires lowering the standards of education. (I read this in the *Tulsa World*).

The article stated that enough education would reduce crime and incarceration. If everyone became a doctor, lawyer, or engineer, there would be no need for Welfare. There would be no more unwed mothers, because the youth would be educated to practice birth control.

Society would move toward enlightenment and freedom from crime, drugs, and other social ills—all because of education. (If you are reading this fifty years from today, you know it didn't work out quite that way.)

Since that time some twelve years ago, colleges and universities have been graduating students who could not even read or write. The grand objective was failing.

Athletics also caused the lowering of educational standards. Colleges and universities began offering just about every incentive they could come up with, including lowered academic requirements, to attract excellent football athletes for an all-star winning team.

It is clear that football stars do not have to read and write to succeed. Barry Sanders and other athletes have earned millions of dollars in the sports arena. They earn more money than they can ever use. What's left then?

The *Tulsa World* reported on one incredibly good player who could catch the ball no matter what. He graduated from high school in Georgia. This guy could command the moon and sixpence for playing football. However, he also wanted to be a doctor, deeming this a more respected career. So the professors took him to a hospital and allowed him to watch a surgical procedure.

Due to the lowered academic requirements, the fellow decided it wasn't necessary to complete med school and actually assumed he was a qualified surgeon. After all, he had seen the procedure.

I don't know if the "doctor" was ever allowed to set up practice. I think he was on the right track though. Even if he became a highly-paid professional athlete instead, it's important for a guy to have a profession of some kind to fall back on. What if he receives a permanent injury? Then what?

I suppose he might go into the music industry. That career has its own hazards. I saw a well-known recording star on a TV show the other night, and his good looks were gone. It was easily discernible that he was on drugs, heavy. One of the songs he wrote described how many highs he had been on.

He died soon after that recording.

With all the education we have warning young people against them, addictive drugs still have a stronghold in every strata of society.

Man has an insatiable craving for something and tries to satisfy it in fame, success, or fortune. Enough education could possibly get him all three; however, he eventually finds this is not enough. Then he turns to drugs.

How about grass? Good for awhile. But soon he tires of grass. He needs a bigger high, a bigger thrill. He tries cocaine.

That was a charge. What a sensation.

Is there something higher?

The flesh is never satisfied.

When he runs out of highs, what's left? The ultimate high? Is that death?

Count the famous entertainers you know who have killed themselves by overusing drugs. They had everything, had every high, and they had nothing.

They did not discover there is Someone higher.

Moral of the story: Be sure to ask for the doctor's medical transcript before submitting to treatment. If universities and those in academia have lowered standards too much, you may want to reconsider.

A good doctor can cure many ills, however society's worst ills cannot be cured by education.

Aging Is Grand,
But Not For Sissies

I have been improving from spinal surgery and expect to make a full recovery by summer, after which I will go swimming at Carlton Lake, unless they prohibit any person over age 70 to swim without a life jacket. It's bad enough to have to swim in a pool with the water dyed yellow so no one my age feels discriminated against if they accidentally "add" to the color.

I have been trying to round up some protestors, but so far the guys I've approached can't walk any farther than the front yard, or else the Quinton Nursing Home won't release them. One old guy said he didn't want to go swimming. Said it was bad enough having to take a shower once a month whether he needed it or not.

A wizened old lady with a poof of white dandelion-wisp for hair got all fired up talking about the bathing beauty contest she won back in 1936. Said she could win another one if they held it for her age group, which is over 80. She boasted that she looks good in yellow, so the dyed water wouldn't bother her much.

Then the others decided it would be fun to hold an old timers' rodeo. They held try-outs and a crowd gathered at the Quinton arena, but not one old timer showed up. Not even the famous barrel-racing Green sisters, Beth and Nancy, who wouldn't have qualified as old anyway. Not for a long time yet.

One wrinkled old fellow finally arrived. He was in a wheelchair and had a stick horse with him. He thought it was an actual living horse and cautioned people not to come near for fear it would kick them in the shinbone, even though he was holding a tight rein on it.

Now all you young people should know this. Don't fear the ravages of old age. It's not for sissies, that's true. But your best years are always just ahead of you.

Yes, they really are.

I know an old guy who doesn't like to wear his hearing aid because every time he turns a page in the newspaper it sounds like the Chicago fire. Having a hearing problem is not a criminal act. If you have a handicap of any kind, learn to live with it, whether it is your hearing or maybe your spouse. Hope for the best. Trust in the future. Believe things will improve.

I look forward to the seasons. As soon as one is over, there's another just ahead, each with its own rewards. An abundance of past does not imply a shortage of future.

We mostly like our looks and don't wish to lose them, but the river of time moves on, and we have to go along with it. Of course some people (like myself) stay handsome as they age.

My sister, Ada, sent me a card. She wrote, "I always looked forward most to supper time. The work is done. The table is set for the evening meal with the family. There's fun and rest to follow."

I never knew Ada could write.

There is a new melody going around. It's called, "I Like Grandpa Jones." I don't know if there are any words to it yet, but I hear people humming it wherever I go.

How about this for lyrics?

Life begins at seventy five.
Jumping Jeepers, man alive!

Will Rogers Had It Right
(This story appears in a May, 2009 edition of the Rockford Labor News)

Oklahoma's best-known philosopher and comedian Will Rogers once said, "If General Motors and Standard Oil Companies were turned over to our senators and congressmen, they would each be bankrupt in less than two years."

I've long believed this myself. Will's comment was meant as a joke when he said it, but millions now consider it all too seriously.

Our seemingly inexhaustible revenue from law makers and "legal" spenders keeps our government's bills paid one way or the other, mostly by reaching into the pockets of taxpayers for more each time they've squandered the first take.

I got to thinking ahead, say a few years from now. In order to curb inflation or recession and to make certain consumers get a fair deal, the government takes over not only the auto industry, but the oil and gas companies too.

So I go to buy a car. What happens?

First, I must apply for an order from my state senator. Then I mail it to Ford or General Motors, whichever one is not already bankrupt. I'm not allowed to walk into an actual show room until the order has been processed.

Four months later, I get a card saying, "Your order is being processed."

Wonderful!

I tell my wife, and we decide not to have any repair work done on the old car parked in our driveway. We call the commissioner who sends a tow truck to haul it to the Reconstruction Auto Lot. There it will be completely rebuilt and placed for sale on the Recycled Transportation website.

At least the old heap is out of my way. Oh yeah, I received a check for $20. My car was actually valued at a thousand, but by the time I paid the moving, handling, recycling and title work fees, the thousand bucks had dwindled.

So now I'm afoot, but my new auto should be ready any day. The letter finally arrives. "Your order has been processed, and you are eligible for a new car. Just fill out the enclosed questionnaire and send it back as soon as possible."

What? I thought we had filled out the order form with our preferences. Now we are informed the body style, model, color, and tire choices are standardized for purposes of equality for all. All cars are now olive-drab with numerous green-fuel-only and non-toxic emission controls and safety features which have lowered the vehicle's standard performance to six miles per gallon.

Okay, fine. I'll take it. I fill out the questionnaire again. I see no purpose in this meaningless exercise, since all cars are now standardized, exactly the same, but I do it since I need transportation.

Another month goes by. I'm driving my farm tractor to the grocery store. Then another letter arrives informing me that the standard series I ordered has been discontinued. "You are advised that the vehicle you wish to purchase will be replaced by the latest standard auto for all Americans. Fill out the enclosed form."

I fill out the form; glad to see the uniform olive-drab body paint is now pea green. After another month, I get my notice and a walk-in order date. Happy day. I make a trip to the nearest Auto Distribution Department and present my papers, I.D. card and fill out additional necessary forms.

The receptionist says I should be seated while they check my file folder. Clerks are everywhere dressed in pea-green uniforms. One brings me coffee. I admire the surroundings. At noon, I'm advised to return around one p.m. I decide to get some lunch.

By two in the afternoon, I'm finally cleared through securities and ushered back to the production department. Soft music is piped into the building, but no one can understand the singer's language. The workers are distributed along the assembly line according to height. It seems shorter people don't wish to be discriminated against by being stationed next to a co-worker of taller stature.

The workers also are positioned so that every assembly line is identical. First in line is always a black man, followed by a white female, then a Hispanic man, followed by a black female, etc. It must have taken months to select these hundreds of workers with the appropriate ethnic background, height, gender, etc.

I watch the assembly of my car as it moves along the line. Finally it rolls off the conveyor belt at the end and the last bolt is tightened. A young lady in the pea-green uniform hands me the keys. I have all my papers in order and I'm ready to roll when an alarmed voice announces over the intercom: "Attention. Please hold all 106 A Models. The flams have been found faulty and the zerts have not been included to provide proper control of toxic-fume emissions from the ziggs or the frumps."

I call my wife to say I'll be catching a train for home. "It's going to be awhile before our new Model 106 A is ready."

"Well that's okay, honey," she answers. "The refineries are still hiring size, gender, and height matching employees for their production lines. They won't be producing enough fuel to drive a car for the next eight months anyway."

In Good Company

In the year of Lord, 1991, I Jones Barnett take pen in hand to state the following disclaimer: (That's the old style of letter writing. Anyway I got the formalities over with.)

Because my kids and grandkids all enjoyed a spine-tingly story, I took the time to spin these tales. I'm also in good company. The following was told by a fellow named F. Scott Fitzgerald, who became a widely recognized author.

According to Fitzgerald, the year was 1926 when two Princeton University students were talking one evening. One of them said, "Do you know how to enter your room at night without being bothered by a ghost?"

The listener thought this was the beginning of a joke.

The talker continued. "First you get a long stick. Then open the door to your room, but stand back. As the door swings open, shove the stick through and swing it around quickly for several strokes. Then you can go inside safely enough, but don't get close to your bed or the ghost could reach out and grab your ankle.

"So now you take the stick and thrust it under the bed for a good many strokes. Then you can get into your bed safely enough. The ghost won't bother you once you're in bed."

Those were Fitzgerald's actual comments on ghostly visitors. He was considered a literary genius, but perhaps I tell a better ghost story. My kids and grandkids think so too. And after all, they are the ones I most want to entertain.

If they find the stories in this book amusing, I shall be most satisfied.

A New Day
It's after midnight.
The moon arises.
It's very slow.
Not yet in view, I see its amber glow.
It comes now suddenly over the trees.
Time moves quickly, a rapid pace.
I'll see but once this view from here, but never more
your face.
And just above it now a star—it's very dim, an eter-
nity away.
Could we but pass this way again? I think perhaps we
may.
An endless sleep, ten million years, and wake re-
freshed
And see once more with knowledge from today re-
tained,
And meet, and recognized at last,
Start once more the sweet refrain and play
The melody through again.

6

Editor's note: Naomi Boggs says Harriett inherited her Dad's flare for telling a story or writing a poem. Since she encouraged me (and since I'm the editor of this historic book) I have included a few of my own attempts on the following pages.

We Can Dream, Can't We?

Dreams are the flavor, the color, the frosting,
Maybe even what keeps the balloon floating.
Anyone can pop a balloon.
Only a dreamer can make one float again.

The Question

When on the whispering wind's euphony
Midnight's melodious night creatures weave
Woodland refrains in a sweet harmony,
Then do I ponder the long mystery—
Who's the composer of this
Symphony?

Shimmering moonlight on pale lilac mist,
Twinkling glow worms on meadows dew kissed,
What painter's brush with a touch and a twist
Painted this midsummer's amorous
Tryst?

Without the answer life surely consists
Of paintings and symphonies forever
Missed.

Psalm 19: I. "The heavens declare the glory of God and the earth shows His handiwork."

Editor's note: I like words that paint pictures. I included these lines because they follow the theme of Jones' book, a universal longing for life beyond the Vail.

"The Fool Hath Said. . ."

"There is no God," I said, and then I plowed my fertile fields.
The golden sun and crystal rain produced a wondrous yield.
Emerald became amber hay for hungry-cattle feed.
T'was not my hand brought forth the gifts that life has borne.
I plowed the field and sewed the seed. I could not make the corn.
And now I watch the setting sun go down in scarlet flames,
And hope that like the faithful sun I too will rise again.

(Written for a doubter)

"The fool says in his heart there is no God. An even greater fool discovers God and then fails to serve Him."-Anonymous

A Writer's Prayer

"I will write a lovely poem to the King." Psalms 45:1

Be Thou the Author, Lord, not me.
Here are the empty pages of my life.
Write upon them Thy perfect will.
Those already filled by me have many errors.

I couldn't cover them completely
With the white-out of correction.
I tried, but they remained.

Then I learned forgiveness is written with
Indelible Lamb's blood, blotting out the
Handwriting of the ordinances against me.

Those smudged and dirty pages now are clean!
Write upon these empty pages
Thy perfect poetry.
Be Thou Author and finisher, O Lord,
Not me.

Editor's note:

Like my father, I can escape from wintry chills through the warm, colorful landscapes of imagination called to mind by vivid words. But sooner or later, the fires die down. Reality has a way of intruding.

1987 Written on returning from a brief respite from the deep freeze in Illinois. . .

Back to Snowy Rockford From Florida

A fuchsia globe sinks into a silver sea
Pink and purple haze. . . then turquoise sky
Fades to indigo.
Tropical breezes blow
Where only a moment before
Was *snow.*
I can escape winter's icy breath,
But only in my mind.
Still that's not a bad place to dwell.

Elegant palm fronds bow.
Children splash in turquoise pools.
Seagulls dip and circle, hoping for crumbs.

And my fire needs tending.

Lost Wealth
"Of all the words put down by pen, the saddest of these, it might have been."—Anonymous

The course of a life can turn dramatically on a single happening. A sharp turn in the life of Marion Barnett (yes, the Civil-War rascal himself) happened as told below.

Jones and his younger sister, Naomi, told two versions of the following.

After the war years, Marion owned prosperous acreage in Missouri. When he made a cattle drive to Lebanon, several neighbors near the settlement of Competition, Missouri sent a few of their cattle along.

The sale went well. The cashier behind a barred window at the crowded sale barn was passing out bundles of cash to ranchers eager to get on their way home. Marion reached for his payment, but before he could pick up the money from the counter, a hand darted out from the pressing crowd. In an instant, the money was gone.

Surrounded by men, Marion was unable to identify the thief. He had to ride home without his hard-earned sum, probably a year's wages at the time.

An honorable man pays his debts, and Marion was an honorable man. In order to pay his neighbors for their cattle, he sold his property and moved his family to another state.

Naomi's version of this story is that Marion was asleep in camp and the thief rolled him during the night.

One cannot help wondering what would have happened to the Barnett family if they had remained on their prosperous Missouri land.

Eventually, Marion's son Charles and wife Josie Barnett settled on a farm near Kinta, Oklahoma where they raised five children: Mary (Snow), Ada (McBride), Jones Barnett, Lucy (Terpening), and Naomi (Boggs).

A similar tale of lost wealth happened on Christine (Iness) Barnett's side of the editor's family.

Jones' wife, Christine, says her grandfather, Elias Fulsom, was farming and raising a family south of Kinta at the time. He began to suffer health problems and decided to drive his cattle to a sale in Fort Smith where he received a tidy sum of money.

When Elias started home, weary and unwell, he grew apprehensive, convinced he was being followed. He caught a ferry on the Canadian River and rode as far as Tomaha, hoping to elude his pursuer. It was dark as he got off the boat.

Elias set out walking through the thick woods. Behind him a shadowy figure moved from tree to tree. In his weakened condition, Elias knew he would be unable to handle a fight. He decided to bury his money, thinking he'd return later and dig it up.

Unfortunately, the illness overtook him. Elias died shortly after making his way home.

The Fulsom family never knew where he had buried their much-needed money.

What might have been?

It's a question we all ask from time to time when looking back. There are no answers.

Only stolen or buried treasure, probably best forgotten.

"For where your treasure is, there your heart will be also." Matt. 6:21.

I Almost Landed
The Landers Job

April, 1987

Dear Ann Landers:
The chance of a lifetime has come and gone. I won't be sitting in your former desk at the *Sun Times* after all.
Signed,
Once-aspiring Advice Columnist, Harriett Ford

On March 13, 1987, Matthew Storin, editor of the *Chicago Sun Times,* mailed out 108 FedEx letters congratulating hopeful advice columnists who were competing for Ann Landers' vacant position. On April 5th, Storin sent 80 letters of regret. I got one of each.

The first letter I put in my album filled with First-Place honors and writing awards. (*Somewhat* filled. . . okay it was empty at the time.)

The second letter went into the trash. Who wants to keep a letter that starts with the words "Bad news"? I get enough of that when my girls bring home their latest boyfriends.

Out of 11,000 people who answered the *Sun Times* ad for Ann Landers' replacement, (because she had moved to the *Tribune*) one person will have the chance of a lifetime. Unfortunately, that person will not be me.

Ann Landers and her sister Abby both started at the *Sun Times* and have become America's most popular advice columnists. Feature editor Scott Powers says "We're hoping to make it happen again."

As a free-lance writer, I have had some experience with rejection. Slight experience. It was quite devastating the one time it happened, however I soon realized one editor's rejection is not final. The next editor may grab up my act of literature with enthusiasm. It has happened. I won't say how often, but enough to show me there is no end to hope . . . unless Hope wanted to be the next Ann Landers.

I gave the competition my best shot. I answered the four sample questions with humor, contemporary wit and wisdom, and compassion. I got editorial advice from two respected writers in my hometown newspapers' offices. I labored over just the right, pert-and-pithy definition of the word *chutzpah*, (one of my questions) debating between "a self-made man who worships his creator," and "*Chutzpah*, much like its French relative *Faux Pas*, can bloody well happen in British. Deliberate audacious gall is never restricted to Yiddish."

I polished, perfected, and prayed. After my answers were mailed, I determined not to think *what if. . .*but the what-ifs continued to enter my mind like a pesky fly that can't be shooed away. I could not help seeing my present circumstances through different-colored glasses. What was more-than-satisfactory before suddenly appeared common, dull, tarnished. The pot of gold at the end of the rainbow was visible, almost within reach.

My vanity showed me pictures of myself appearing on television interviews, speaking and lecturing, writing books that publishers would grab up greedily.

My practical self said, "Shut-up. Who would want your opinion anyway?"

My home-making self said, "Wow! You could replace your worn out carpet."

My inflated ego said "Your husband will sit up and take notice of your writing efforts now, not to mention Mom, Dad, and all the friends and relatives."

My mother's heart said "But your two daughters need you. You don't want to get yourself into a demanding schedule that would cause you to neglect them."

Ambition unfortunately, has a louder voice than Martyrdom. I could not seriously see myself turning the column down. Of course, now that I won't have that option, I can always pretend I might have. I can tell myself that all that glitters is not gold. There will be other rainbows.

My worn out carpet will last another year.

I wish the very best to Ann Landers, and the very worst to the guy who tossed my answers in the "out" pile. (Well, not the very worst actually. A paper cut will do.)

I remember reading of a few tired fishermen who caught nothing after a long night. Jesus told them to let down their nets again. It's time to get out my typewriter and go fishing.

True, the big one got away, but that never stopped a real fisherman.

Editor's note:

Harriett was soon employed by *Rockford Labor News*, a weekly newspaper in Rockford, Illinois, where she has written a popular advice/humor column **Sara and Sadie's Sense and Nonsense** for over twenty years.

Turning Forty

By Harriett Barnett Ford

(Written a just a couple of years ago.)

Reprint (Appearing in June '87 of RIGHT HERE, THE HOMETOWN MAGAZINE, Indiana.)

The Statue of Liberty and I have something in common. We both had a birthday in July. She had a face-lift and I didn't. She's sixty years older than I, but she's an old maid. I've survived twenty years of marriage.

I've been through bobby socks in the sixties, mini-skirts in the seventies, and new-wave-punk in the eighties. She hasn't changed her dress in a hundred years.

I've been through brush rollers, hot rollers, curling irons, blow cuts, frizzy perms, feathered bangs, and mousse. Miss Liberty hasn't changed her hair-do at all.

I've raised two beautiful daughters, a Siamese cat, dogs, and hamsters, and also several neighbors' kids. Lady Liberty has never changed a diaper.

Having the benefit of these experiences qualifies me to say something. The inescapable fact that I am not only grown up, but also growing older, makes me want to commit to paper some of my vast wisdom and observations on life. (Not the "sum." That would take at least three pages.)

I have great respect for my great-grandmothers who made it through life without Teflon, television, microwaves, mixers, Maybeline, many unmentionables, and McDonalds. Without them I wouldn't be here. (Without my grandmothers that is.) I'm sure they would have relevant information to share with women of the eighties. I should like very much to read their observations on turning forty. That brings me to my first observation. Information is the key to making wise decisions. (After all, I'm a serious voter now.) Never vote for a candidate without knowing what office he's running for.

Having been married for exactly half my life, I have made the following monumental discoveries.

Marriage...

I recommend it highly, especially if one is considering motherhood.

Many of my contemporaries are going through their second marriage, divorce, or nervous breakdown. I'm still on my first (marriage that is), and its rough spots are getting smoothed out. He used to do things that drove me "bananas". He still does the same things, but they don't bother me anymore.

Some things are worth dying for, but *very* few things are worth arguing over.

Being right at the risk of damaging a relationship is usually wrong.

Don't assume your husband can read your mind. Ask a specific question if you really want an answer. "Where are you taking me to dinner?" instead of "What do you want for dinner tonight?" should get the proper results.

Love is not a feeling. It is an action. Mostly a giving action. Be more concerned with giving than receiving.

Love that demands something in return will likely fail. Love overcomes all things, but human love is very frail. It won't go far unless it taps into an endless supply. That only comes from God, for God is love.

Motherhood...

It's a lifetime position.

Sisters need time alone with mother. Time when they do not have to compete with each other for her attention.

One Cabbage-Patch doll is never enough.

Never give children a choice of where to eat or what to eat for that matter. Simply say, "We're going to McDonalds for hamburgers." You will save enough time to write a book otherwise spent on arguing.

In an active family of four, eating a sit-down dinner is a rare occasion. (Especially since I don't cook everyone's favorite meals every night, or even once a week).

Childhood forms the habits of a lifetime. Even though I am persuaded nothing more sinister than a dust bunny lurks under my bed, I still don't sleep with my hands or feet hanging off my bed. (I doubt my cousin Nancy does either.) Make it a habit to instill in children the perfect love which casts out fear.

Age...

Most people don't believe they look as old as they are. Never ask people to guess your age or weight.

Clairol and Oil-of-Olay may help a sagging morale, but only in imagination. A whistle from the guys helps a whole lot. (I got whistled at once last year and haven't changed my hair style since.)

I have lived long enough to know I'm never going to be a Julia Childs cook. I've learned that most men don't eat Jell-O-salads, casseroles, or quiche. Husbands will eat them, but they have a way of preferring something else. (I don't know what it is, because I've never prepared it yet.)

I have accepted the fact that I'm never going to have a Barbie-doll figure. My figure has Barbie's same bumps, only more of them and in different places.

Older people are younger than they used to be.

Old friends really are *old* friends.

The most ordinary events can now produce the most extraordinary pleasure. The high point of the week is a dull evening at home.

Nobody cares that I was Valedictorian in high school.

My twentieth class reunion has come and gone, like the promises of youth, all fulfilled or forgotten.

We spent the time looking back, talking of what we did rather than what we are going to do. Most achieved their goals: Roy Perryman, Betty Ross, Beth Green, Bill Carter, Larry Holt. Some found contentment raising their families in or near Kinta's small community. Ramona Reasnor, C. B. Coplen, Nelda Carter (actually Nelda was a year behind my class.)

Members of every graduating class have a few great successes and probably a few great failures.

Which is more tragic? Wasted youth or wasted potential?

Fashion...

I can wear my daughter's shoes.

My daughter can wear my clothes (but only the ones that are not old fogey). Some of my clothes are older than my kids! I guess those are the old fogey ones.

Being liberated is when taste is more a matter of personal preference than what fashion dictates. I reserve the right to wear autumn's colors even if I am classified as a winter.

The need to be unique is universal. The need to conform also is universal.

How does one be a unique conformist without being a rebel? Or an extremist? Or unfashionable? It's easy if you happen to be the Statue of Liberty.

Lady Liberty and I have something else in common. We are both beautiful, even though she had a face-lift and I didn't. The secret of her beauty lies in the sweet dream of liberty she represents. The secret of mine is that I know where it's at. Liberty that is.

"For where the Spirit of the Lord is, there is liberty." **(2nd Cor. 3:17).**

Like Mother used To Make

(words to make a bride groan)

Of all things said about the cake.
Unkindest were the words,
"It's not like mother used to make."
I wish I hadn't heard.
Like mother used to make indeed!
Of course not, you forget,
Mixes, Teflon, micro-waves were not invented yet.
But just to please my gourmet groom,
I baked a cake from scratch.
No mixes. Nothing artificial
Went into the gooey batch.
It had the strangest sunken place,
The center was a pool of runny frosting poured thereon
Before the cake was cool.
I stood with rolling-pin in hand and dared him criticize
my cake.
"Why, Darling," said he, "this is grand."

"It's just like Mother used to make!"

7

The Rejection
When my lovely prose creation
Is returned, no compensation,
I can bridle my frustration
By one simple consolation—
Tell myself this prose creation
Shall increase the circulation
Of a finer publication!
(What a senseless occupation!)

This was written for my son-in-law, Darin, after his engagement to my daughter.

1989

To You Who Kissed My Daughter...

You kissed her, not a stolen kiss, nor hidden.
A kiss that from her lips was freely given.
Her heart is only hers to give as well,
A gift whose value God alone can tell,
For she was fashioned by His loving hand.
And I will trust that one who understands
that touching lips to lips is but a part
of tenderness that manifests love's art.
For love is something you receive by giving.
The greater part of love is in forgiving.

May God bestow His blessings on the man
who kisses her within His perfect plan.

(The above poem is an unfinished sonnet.
Someone please add two more lines).

Who Gives This Woman?

Must I give her now to you who never loved her as I do?
Empty hands that rocked her cradle held her little hand once too.
Led her through the rites of passage from a baby to a bride.

Not too closely nor too loosely, take her hand and by your side
Lead her gently, lead her always with Our Father as your Guide.

Smiling, he replied,

Her cradle's long been empty and her hand that once was small
Is no longer weak and tiny. God is leading. We won't fall.
We have pledged to love each other. Time will tell our love is true.
So I'll take her now from you who cannot love her as I do.

(Written for Darin Ramlow, who must remember the above when some young man asks for his daughter's hand one day.)

Jones And Harriett Travel
To Spook Light Road

Editor's note: Jones and Harriett did indeed visit Spook Light Road. Following is the story which has appeared in more than one publication.

Spoooooky!

Everyone loves a good mystery with a touch of the supernatural, and the hills of Oklahoma have their share. Residents of Hornet Missouri and Quapaw, Oklahoma are accustomed to thrill seekers driving to the area to see the famous "spook light," a mysterious and unexplainable light which has been raising goose bumps for over a hundred years.

There's got to be an explanation, but researchers have yet to find it. One of the popular theories, that it's a reflection of headlights, doesn't stand up because the Osage and Quapaw Indians reported seeing it long before the advent of automobiles. Farmers also saw it during horse and buggy days.

The Army Corps of Engineers has studied it. Teams of scientists have written about it in numerous publications.

(I have a lot of confidence in scientists. They've discovered that a Queen bee can give precise directions, however the male worker bees *refuse* to ask for them. I could have told them that.)

Over the years, at least one fellow claimed the spook light burned him. If that's true, it lends credence to the theory of the light being an atmospheric electrical pulse caused by shifting rocks. Seismic activity. The area along the mystery light's path has been known for earthquakes. Four quakes happened along the New Madrid fault line during the 18th century alone.

Dad said he didn't want to be the only person in the U.S. and Canada who hadn't seen the phenomenon. I wanted to see the light myself, ever since my unexpected encounter with a UFO. (More on that later. I don't believe in alien craft visiting earth, but I'm one of the 45 million people world-wide who has seen an unidentified flying object.).

During the drive from my Dad's place in Kinta, I had purchased a sensational tabloid (just for fun) and was reading about a marauding killer rooster on the rampage.

"Better keep our windows rolled up," I said. "A marauding killer rooster might leap in and flog us to death."

"The world needs its mysteries," Dad answered. "Too much reality is hard on the soul."

Dad is a guy who enjoys mysteries as much as the next guy. He raises serious questions such as: If Dracula can't see himself in the mirror, how come his hair is always so neatly combed? And what do the angels say to God if He sneezes?

The sun was setting when we found the four-mile stretch of country road about twelve miles southwest of Joplin. The lane actually crosses the Oklahoma border through a dip in the hills toward Quapaw.

Thick woods lined both sides of the road, their branches lifted like silent sentinels holding bayonets in a shadowy archway overhead.

There were a few cars parked on the road side, thrill seekers come to view the spectacle—or simply to view each other. We rolled down the window of the car and pulled up beside a Chevy van.

"You here to see the spook light too?" I greeted a middle-age couple who looked sane enough. They grinned.

"We've seen it lots of times. I'm Ralph Younkers and this is Bonnie. We live in Joplin. Sometimes we stop by this road when we're driving through the area, just to see if the light is doing anything different."

"What do you think it could be?"

"I think it's a beacon for a UFO," said Bonnie. "Some people claim they saw one near the corner by Spooky Joe's old place. That used to be a museum of sorts, but it's shut down now."

We talked with the Younkers while the shadows deepened. They described the light. "It's the size of a basketball and spins down this gravel road at high speeds, sometimes just bouncing up and down or weaving from side to side. No one can ever get close to it when they try. It's in front of them one minute, and the next it's behind them," said Ralph.

Bonnie added, "People say they can feel heat from it."

She had exited the Chevy and was examining a patch of wild sweet peas and black berries along the road side.

A whippoorwill called from nearby. Ralph commented, "This road gets real crowded on weekends. People come from everywhere to see it. Course some of them are on drugs or drinking beer. Those guys could see anything and think it was a spook. But the actual light is unmistakable."

Bonnie spoke, "Shhhh. There it is!"

We strained our eyes to see a tiny bluish light blinking far down the read. A motorcycle soon appeared instead of the mystery light. The rider stopped and spoke with us about his own experience.

"I've seen it several times. There're lots of nights it doesn't show up at all. I have a friend who lived out here when he first got married. The light floated into his bedroom one night and scared his bride half silly. They moved to town right away."

We learned that the cyclist was a director of continuing education from a Missouri state college. So far, our sighters were very credible.

I had no doubt that this phenomenon was observable, and probably explainable. Joe Springs of Quinton saw it once and described it to us, saying it was so bright he could have read a newspaper on the night he saw it.

The hours passed. Before midnight we had seen it three times. The sightings turned out to be taillights, a patch of moonlight, and a white cat crossing the road. Dad began to examine rocks in the roadbed, finding them more interesting than watching the dark lane.

"Should we warn the Younkers about the killer rooster before we leave?" I asked Dad, who was tapping a tuneless rhythm with his fingers on the hood of the car, his signal that boredom had set in.

"Looks to me like we're more likely to see a killer rooster than a spook light," he answered.

We drove back to Kinta, a little disappointed that the light had avoided us.

But our sense of mystery was not lost. Especially when a gorgeous full pumpkin moon rose over the hills, and a falling star or comet seemed to follow our car.

Or could it have been . . .?

A Step Beyond
(My UFO Sighting)

If a zombie had lumbered up and slapped me in the face I couldn't have been more surprised.

I never expected such an event and would not have believed it until it happened to me.

Do I dare admit that I've actually become one of "those people?"

Yes. Like most of the 40 million people worldwide who have reported this experience (according to Larry King) I'm compelled, regardless of the consequences.

I have indeed seen a UFO.

It was rather an unforgettable occurrence, but will it shatter my worldview?

Isn't that the real question behind such a sighting? The challenge to go a step beyond the earth into unknown possibilities? To boldly go where no man has ever gone before? (In my case, that's the Ladies' Room and no farther.)

Despite tons of people who firmly believe intelligent life exists on other planets, I've always maintained a healthy skepticism.

Of course that leaves room for **un**intelligent life in the galaxies, but I figure we have enough of that on our own planet to go around the entire universe.

Here's what happened.

I had stepped out on my front porch in Rockford, Illinois to pick up the morning paper. The sun was rising. The morning jogger was passing by. All was calm as usual on Regal Ridge Circle, including me.

I glanced upwards and there it was, suspended just above the trees in my front yard, as motionless and silent as the silvery moon.

But it was not the moon.

Just for the record, I had already downed one cup of coffee and rubbed the sleep from my eyes.

I looked at the thing with mild curiosity. The jogger wasn't paying any attention. The newspaper boy rode his bicycle away without a shrug. Nobody shouted in horror, "LOOK! THERE'S AN ALIEN CRAFT!" So I stepped back inside, thinking it must be an ordinary occurrence in the neighborhood.

Surely I was not the only one who saw it. Probably just a hot air balloon, I decided.

Who was I kidding?

I *knew* it wasn't a balloon. There was no sound of bellows blowing. No tether. No slogan such as "Eat at Joe's," or "Happy Birthday Martha."

I stepped outside again.

The thing had not moved. It was as big as a water tower and shaped like a giant garbage can. That alone tells you I'm not making this up. Why describe an aerial object that could not possibly fly?

There were no lights, no windows, and no big-eyed, gray dwarves inviting me aboard for a cup of Starbucks.

There was one other very odd feature I won't describe, because if I ever do speak with someone who saw the same feature, I'll know at once he's telling the truth.

By this time, I was intrigued. I scurried to grab my news camera. Yes, I'm a reporter.

It was OUT of film! How could that be?

This was worse than an encounter with a dangerous alien. Worse even than having my hair turn green. I could have sold that photo to every tabloid and newspaper in the country. Been interviewed by Larry King. Made headlines in the *Wacky World News!*

Deep breathely, I said aloud, trying to calm myself.

Of course, like all typical UFOs, the thing had disappeared in the few minutes it took to locate a spare camera. UFOs are notoriously camera shy.

Could something that large have disappeared so quickly without a sound?

Of course not.

I jumped in my Jeep and drove to the top of the nearest hill in the neighborhood, thinking I'd spot it floating lazily away.

It couldn't have vanished into thin air.

Or could it? As far as I could see, that's exactly what happened.

The puzzle nagged at me throughout the day.

Disappointed that I'd missed my chance to sell "Astonishing Photo of the Year," I decided to research mysterious aerial phenomenon and write a feature story, using my own sighting as a springboard.

I discovered that unidentified objects in the heavens are hardly a modern phenomenon. As early as 1504 to 1450 B.C., a historian writing on Egyptian Papyrus in the annals of Thutmose III described circles of fire in the sky, shining more brightly than the sun. The entire army of Pharaoh looked on and witnessed these mysterious orbs ascending higher in the sky and moving toward the south.

The ancient Nazca line drawings in Peru are so large they can only be seen from the air, yet air travel was still thousands of years in the future. Some people attribute their very existence to aliens, just as they ascribe the pyramids to advanced intelligence.

Advanced intelligence indeed. These theories do the ancients a disservice by assuming their architectural wonders were constructed using other-worldly technology. People have always been resourceful, no less ingenious in the past than the present.

My investigation soon led me to the Aerial Phenomenon Research Organization (APRO) based near Byron, Illinois, a center which has studied UFO sightings for decades.

Chicago Dr. Karyn K. Mitchell, Ph. D. was scheduled to speak on how to help people who believe they've been abducted by aliens. I thought her presentation would lend scholarly balance to my UFO feature.

The woman looked professional, confident and self assured. The attendees looked sane and ordinary, sitting pleasantly around a table in a lower room of the school building, an appropriate place for inquiring minds.

I felt reassured.

Then she introduced herself. "I am Dr. Mitchell, and I am an abductee."

Uh oh. She had weirded me out already.

"People who believe they have been abducted are *attuned to a frequency* that's not attainable by the non-abducted society," she explained.

Well, yeah. I could buy that. One visitor to my news office says she communicates with aliens on a different telepathic wave every night. She is also hoping for Bigfoot to appear as her partner on *Dancing With The Stars.*

Dr. Mitchell said she is "led by a Universal Consciousness to help abductees to freedom." She described a race called the Zeta Reticuli, which are intent on medical experiments with earthlings.

Medical experiments? That might be a good thing if they can they lower cholesterol and help get rid of HMOs.

Unfortunately, Zetas are solely interested in breeding with earthlings.

This was puzzling. Instead of going to the trouble of abductions, I wondered why they wouldn't just visit a sperm bank and make a withdrawal. (I've always thought the same about vampires and blood banks.)

I kept quiet.

Dr. Mitchell described using hypnotherapy to help clients recall their abduction experiences.

She spoke of karma, Cosmic Ashtar Affiliates, the Higher Good, Buddha's realms corresponding to seven heavens, Ascended Masters—the woman was a believer in a whole conglomerate of Divine Essences and Dark Forces.

I had to leave the meeting early, afraid I was going to burst into cosmic gales of laughter—not at the sincere Dr. Mitchell or her convinced colleagues.

The entire subject was so bizarre, so alien (a bad pun?) a giant step beyond my comfort zone. I'm an armchair traveler who dreams of going places, but my armchair stays firmly grounded. Space travel appeals to me only at the thought of weightlessness in space.

I drove back to Rockford through an eerie night, blacker than the space of Hades. (That's blacker than the ace.)

Safely home without a single alien encounter, I sat down to think about the facts. As a news reporter, I know very well that facts can be distorted or misinterpreted.

I know what I saw was unexplained.

I also know there is an explanation. The floating-garbage-can thing was a hot-air balloon after all. It popped and that's why it seemed to vanish.

Worldviews are difficult to change. If people don't want to believe in alien visitors, they cannot be stopped. Just as believers cannot be unconvinced. Don't bother "those people" with any facts.

I decided to put the whole subject on the shelf, however, for months, each time I walked out my front door, I couldn't help glancing up to see if the balloon reappeared.

Still, I knew it was not a balloon.

Eventually I opened the Bible for ultimate truth. Why not go to the Creator to solve the mysteries of creation? Someone has said that faith is necessary to get to Heaven, but doubt about things in the world gets one an education. It took some reading, but I found answers there.

Later, my husband and I moved to the rural hills of Missouri where it's rumored a Bigfoot creature roams the woods. Some UFO buffs believe Bigfoot is a sub-species, sent down from an alien craft to mutilate cows. Is this logical? Could be. I've never seen an alien ordering his beef from a drive-through window at Wendy's. (Well now that I think of it, I may have seen one or two.)

Speaking of logic, I did not leave mine on the front porch during my close encounter with a UFO. I still do not believe extra terrestrials are visiting the earth.

However, Bigfoot showed up in my yard the other day and asked me if he had any messages. I told him to phone home.

Editor's note: The following story won First Place in the Springfield, MO Sleuth's Ink mystery writer's competition. It is also included in an Ozark's Writer's League (OWL) 2009 anthology.

Unprepared
By Harriett Ford

Ava heard it again.

The sound of footfalls in the hall where there should have been no sound.

She didn't have to strain her ears to know that someone was creeping down the hall toward her bedroom...

Crazy Sam!

Had he actually dared to enter her home this time?

She had discovered the boot prints on her wrap-around porch twice this week alone. It was not a welcome thought to know that he had been there, perhaps spying on her.

Before this afternoon's cloudburst, Ava had found the same prints in the yard once again near her back windows. Clearly Sam's prints. She recognized the slash-marked heel. Sam walked by her mailbox, muttering to himself, at least once a week on his way to town.

Of course Ava had been curious but not overly alarmed by her only nearby neighbor, a former NASA scientist who had suffered a meltdown and retired in the Ozarks to write murder mysteries.

A teller at the Village Bank had assured her Sam was harmless. He'd earned the "Crazy" title because of his hat and the way he preferred to walk everywhere he went, even the three miles from his place to the nearest country store.

"He uses his walking time to plot murder mysteries," the teller explained with a shrug. "I know he looks weird, always wearing that silly carnival hat with the hands waving where the ears ought to be. He says it's good for muffling noise, so he can hear his characters' voices. He's very shy, but usually pleasant enough. Just eccentric."

A harmless eccentric. She had accepted that description at the time.

Since finding his prints around her house, she had become uneasy. Who knew what went on inside his damaged mind? What kind of voices did he really hear? Why was he spying on her?

Earlier that day, she had picked up the phone to dial the county sheriff and report Sam as prowler. Unfortunately, the storm had knocked out the telephone lines.

Now the eccentric writer of murder mysteries was inside her house, and she was trapped in the back bedroom with no exit.

Her eyes darted to the telephone. Hoping against hope, she lifted the receiver. Still no dial tone. Her cell phone did not get reception in these hills.

Darn!

She could hear her late husband Harvey's warning. "Women in danger can't think clearly without a plan already in place, so please take precautions. Be prepared."

Harvey, a veteran Chicago cop, had always warned her she should have a plan in case of an intruder. He'd spent his days dealing with bad characters. One of them may just decide to come after him some night.

Ava had expected him to relax after he retired and they moved to their remote farmhouse in the Ozarks hills. Instead, he had purchased a small-caliber handgun and had wanted her to learn how to shoot.

"You're paranoid, my over-protective husband," Ava chuckled. "You're like Don Quixote. You see monsters where there are only windmills."

"All cops are paranoid, my dear," he had answered with his stock phrase. "We have good reason to be."

Now with an intruder in the house, she sharply regretted ignoring his words.

She had to do something. She couldn't just sit here like a scared rabbit waiting for the wolf to attack.

Maybe she could bluff her way out of this.

Thrusting her hand in the pocket of her robe, she extended her fingers forward to imply she had a gun. Immediately, she thought better of it.

What am I going to say? Stick'em up or I'll let you have it with both fingers?

Ava might have laughed at herself if her heart had not been pounding like the blades of a runaway helicopter.

She'd read a few of Sam's short stories out of curiosity. The man's imagination was muddy with murder and mayhem. What if he wanted to act out one of them now?

She held her breath as the doorknob started turning in slow motion.

I've got to fight this, but how?

Instinctively she reached for anything she might hurl at him. Her hand clutched a pink, knit house slipper.

What am I going to do? Slam him over the head with this? She thought to herself in dismay.

A totally crazy thought.

Crazy. That's it!

Seizing on a desperate plan, Ava grabbed the knitted slipper and stretched it over the top of her head, the toe pointed down her nose. Then she called out with feigned boldness, "Well don't just stand there, Star Man. Come on in! I've been watching your space ship fly over the house every night. I knew you'd come."

If I can convince Sam I'm just a little crazier than he is . . . criminals don't hurt crazy people, do they? She tried to assure herself.

Ava's mind raced ahead, grabbing for a convincing pretense. She recalled phrases from a recent television show she had chanced to see.

"I knew you'd get my telepathic message. Come on in!"

After a long moment, the door swung wide and a hulking frame stood limned in the glow of a hall light.

No hands appeared on the cap in place of ears, but that didn't mean this was not Crazy Sam. The general shape and posture was the same. Besides, Sam would hardly wear something so recognizable if he were going to commit a crime. The mystery writer was far too clever for that.

Wasn't he?

Her every instinct was to dash madly past the figure and run for help, but instead she forced herself to say, "Oh good, you're not one of the Lizard men!"

She attempted a conversational, chatty tone, hoping to disguise the terrible pounding in her chest.

Peering intently, she strived to recognize Sam's features, but the intruder's face was hidden in shadows.

"I can see you're not a Zeta. They're ugly. One of them came here last month. Ate up everything in my pantry."

The figure remained motionless.

Ava felt a whisper of hope. At least he wasn't rushing at her with a knife. She forgot the UFO jargon and decided to invent some of her own.

"Which planet are you from? I've visited Orion. It's a gorgeous planet. Oh yes, I just love the implant they put in my brain! Gives me amazing abilities."

She managed a nervous chuckle that sounded more like a mad cackle.

Fine. The madder the better.

Shadow Man did not approach her.

Keep talking, she encouraged herself, beginning to hope.

"The implant super charges all my senses. Even my night vision is sharp."

He said nothing so she continued the chatter, her pink slipper bobbing over her nose.

"Speaking of super vision, I can see from here that you look pale. Is that your natural color?" She bluffed, unable to see his face in the dark.

The prowler stifled a sneeze.

"Oh, I knew it! You've got galactic fever. Your eyes are yellowish too."

"Lady, you're crazy!" the figure exclaimed.

She had never heard Sam speak so the voice was not a clue.

"Crazy? Not yet. But I could be if the implant wears off. Might just shoot up the countryside or something. Failed implants can turn people into terrorists and cannibals, you know. But don't you worry. If I kill anyone I'll be polite about it. I'll apologize first."

He coughed, and then scoffed, "You really believe aliens are implanting stuff in peoples' brains?"

"Makes the news everyday," she answered the coughing scoffer.

Speaking as if sharing a privileged confidence, she declared, "Those Olympic athletes? How do you think they can do such marvelous feats? Implants. That's how.

"That's also the reason for all those terrible school shootings we've had recently. Implants wear off and the poor students go berserk. The Orions haven't perfected their devices yet, but mine's been working so far. It's the same model they planted in Hillary Clinton, so that should make you feel safer."

"Crazy as a bat in the chimney flu," The shadow snorted in disgust.

Satisfied that she had convinced him of her lunacy, Ava decided to change tactics. She put a hand to her forehead beneath the slipper's pink toe.

"I don't know what it will feel like if it wears off though. Actually, I've been somewhat warm tonight. Almost feverish. Galactic fever is bad news. It's wiped out whole planets you know."

He didn't answer.

With a sudden inspiration, she added, "They call it Bird Flu here on earth. It's very contagious. That's why I summoned you. I'm so glad you came!"

"Bird Flu!" the shadow exclaimed, a note of alarm in his voice. He sneezed again.

Ava spoke confidentially, "Shhh. The doc doesn't want anyone to know it yet, but there've been three cases confirmed in the Ozarks." She nervously held up four fingers instead of three.

"Three cases of bird flu?"

"Just three so far, but the Doctor says it's going to spread. I think he used the word "pandemic." Thank goodness you got my message. You've brought the vaccine, right? To save our planet? Otherwise, we'll all die."

"Where's your lousy husband?" The shadow growled and coughed again.

"I'm sad to say the Bird Flu killed him," Ava spoke dramatically.

"Poor man. It's a terrible death. Hacking and coughing. Just like you're doing now. You don't feel much pain but you start hallucinating when the fever attacks your brain."

"You're saying Bird Flu killed him?" Shadow Man sounded slightly incredulous, less skeptical.

Ava nodded. "It's terribly contagious if you're exposed, you're certain to get it. Say, I'm feeling sorta dizzy. This couldn't be the flu could it? No, course not. I'd be seeing things like Harvey did. He was talking to Peter Pan right before he died. Course I am talking to an alien right now," she chuckled, "but you're real aren't you?"

No answer. She rambled on, describing imaginary symptoms.

"It's when you start to *see* things that you're the most contagious. If anyone comes near you, they get it too, sometimes immediately. It's really weird how the fever can just pounce on you. You're fine one minute and the next, you're plumb out of your mind! Harvey saw monsters. Deer with donkey heads and humans with rabbit ears. Speaking of monsters, I never saw an alien like that one standing behind you right now. He's uglier than a two-headed pig. Are those tentacles hanging from his chin?"

She pointed past him at the empty hallway, pretending to stare at something grotesque.

Shadow Man glanced over his shoulder also, his posture tensed, like a runner at the starting line.

Wiping her brow, Ava muttered, "I'm so hot I could bury myself in ice. Here, feel my forehead."

She took a wobbly step forward. He stepped back, coughing once more.

"Stay away from me you old bat!"

"Oh my. That cough sounds just like poor Harvey's did right before the end. Do you feel feverish too? Say, how's your vision? You been seeing things that aren't there? Weird creatures? Deformed people?"

A sudden movement at the window drew the man's attention.

He gasped.

Ava glimpsed the strange figure with hands growing from the head where the ears should have been, Crazy Sam's familiar carnival hat silhouetted against pale moonlight.

With a wild shriek, the intruder fled, his heavy footfalls thudding down the hall and across the porch. An engine cranked to life, and tires kicked out gravel as the car sped away.

Ava felt a rush of relief, then caught her breath and walked outside to look for Sam.

He was standing in the moonlight on the back porch.

Sam removed the carnival hat and spoke shyly, eyes downcast.

"I was walking by and saw the car again, Ma'am. The same car that's been driving by your place this week. Coupla' times I walked up on the porch to make sure you were okay. You don't usually have company, and your house was dark, so I stopped to check on your welfare," he mumbled.

"I got his license number." Sam handed her a scrap of note paper. "If everything's okay, I'll be going now."

"Thank you Sam," Ava whispered weakly. "You showed up at the best possible time."

Sam was already moving away.

She locked her doors and grabbed the phone to dial the sheriff. The line was still dead. Catching sight of her reflection in the hallway mirror, Ava laughed. She was still wearing the ridiculous pink-knit slipper stretched over her head with the toe pointed over her nose.

If Sam had noticed her bizarre headgear, he was too much of a gentleman to comment. Or maybe he thought she had a right to wear a hat as silly as his own.

Crazy Sam was no monster after all.

But the other guy? Ava shuddered to think of his intent, remembering how Harvey had always feared reprisal from any criminal he had helped put in prison.

She had not been prepared, but her ruse had worked well enough, especially with Sam's timely appearance.

She whispered to her husband's photograph beside the phone, "Women can't think in a crisis, huh Harvey?"

Maybe she would learn to shoot that gun.

Or maybe just keep the slipper handy.

The Author's Plan

In the scheme of things cosmic, universal, and divine,
Perhaps there's hidden poetry written in each line,
And every life's a masterpiece unfolding with a plot
Of unity and harmony within the Author's mind.

A page of sudden sorrow follows pages filled with mirth,
Unexpected, uninvited, giving Grief untimely birth.
When the scheme is without reason, and the poem
doesn't rhyme,
Perhaps there's hidden harmony somewhere between
the lines.

And of every life submitted to the Author's master plot
There is victory in tragedy within His careful thought.
We can trust the Writer's purpose, we can trust the Au-
thor's plan.
We can trust the pages plotted by the Master's loving
Hand.

"I always looked forward to suppertime."
Jones Barnett

AFTERWORD

Like the unfinished story written by Jones, this book is also a work in progress. Harriett Barnett Ford invites any member of the Barnett family or the Kinta community to contribute a story or bit of family history.

Jones Barnett, 1918-1994, was widely known in the Kinta area as the Haskell County Land Surveyor and also a cattle rancher. After serving in the Army during World War II, Jones married his sweetheart, Christine Iness, and worked as a surveyor for Precision Exploration Seismograph Company a number of years before building a house near Kinta. He had two children, Harriett and Scott. Over the course of his later years, he unknowingly accomplished one of his long-time goals—to write a book.

Harriett Barnett Ford, formerly of Kinta, Oklahoma, found the book saved in a cardboard box, a collection of letters, stories, and essays he had sent to her and to her two daughters. She compiled and edited it with many a smile.

Harriett is a former newspaper reporter, an advice columnist, and a published author whose short stories appear in numerous anthologies. She has written two full-length novels, *Shadow in the Rain* and *Frankly Madame*, currently available in bookstores and on Amazon, and is working on her Beyond Fantasy series.

Visit her website at www.deniedevidence.com and send her a message. She enjoys hearing from readers across the country.

Made in the USA